The Short Story Series

GENERAL EDITOR   JAMES GIBSON

LOVE
SUPERNATURAL
DETECTION
HORROR
SCIENCE FICTION
HUMOUR

Humour

CHOSEN BY
F. E. S. Finn

John Murray

Albemarle Street London

Printed and bound in Great Britain
by Butler & Tanner Ltd,
Frome and London

0 7195 3503 4

CONTENTS

The Flying Goat

What? the man in the saloon said to me, you never heard of Jethro Watkins's flying goat? Well, there was a chap in this town, once, who made himself a pair of straw wings; strapped them on his shoulders, jumped off the top of a house and broke his neck. Then there was another chap who made himself a bicycle with wings; he called it a flycycle, and he flycycled over the top of a precipice and broke his neck. But Jethro Watkins had a flying goat. I don't mean a goat that flew with wings. I mean a goat that flew without wings. And when I say flew I mean flew. I don't mean it jumped over some three-foot railings and flew by mistake. It flew regularly. It flew all over England. Surely, he said, you must have heard of Jethro Watkins's flying goat?

'No,' I told him, 'I never heard of it.'

Well, that's funny, he said. You mean you never heard about the time it flew off the tower at Blackpool?

'No,' I told him, 'I can't say I did.'

No? he said. Then you must have heard about the time it flew fifteen times round the tent in Wombwell's circus?

'No,' I told him, 'I can't say I heard about that either.'

I don't know, he said, I'm sure. It's funny. Nowadays nobody seems to have heard about anything.

'Well, who was this Jethro Watkins?' I said.

Well, in the first place he was a very religious chap, he said. He was in the Salvation Army. Used to play the euphonium. And then he was very fat—weighed fifteen, perhaps sixteen stone—and by trade he was a thatcher—you know what I mean, he thatched roofs and stacks. Always up on a ladder, catching every bit of wind. Well, Jethro told me how what with being a euphonium player and a thatcher and always being concerned with wind one way or another he began to study wind. Up there, on his ladder, he used to see what wind could do—toss birds about, toss whole armsful of straw about, almost lift a roof off before he got it pegged down. You know how powerful a big wind is— blows trees down, even blows houses down. Well, Jethro had been studying all that year before he got this idea of a flying goat.

'And how,' I said, 'did he get this idea of a flying goat?'

Like all big ideas, he said. By accident. Just like that. All of a pop. He saw some posters about a menagerie and one of the items was a flying ape and Jethro went to see it. Well, there wasn't much in it. Just a big grey-looking ape that did a big trapeze jump and they called it flying. Well, Jethro thought it was a swindle. He went home in disgust and he went and stood in his back-yard and looked at his goats. Did I tell you he kept goats? No? Well, he'd kept goats for years—bred and raised them. One of the things that made him such a strong, big fat man was goats' milk. He'd drunk it twice a day for years. And suddenly he had this big idea—a flying goat. If a monkey could fly, why not a goat? And if a man could make money out of a flying ape, why couldn't he make money out of a flying goat? The thatching trade had been going down steadily for years, and just about that time it had got down almost to a standstill. So this idea of a flying goat was a godsend. Providence. According to Jethro's idea it was God stretching down a helping hand.

'Now you're going to tell me,' I said, 'that he taught the goat to fly until it could fly well enough to fly round a circus?'

Well, no, he said. That's what he tried to do. But it didn't come off. He got one of his goats and started to train it in the back-yard— you know, put it first on a beer-barrel and made it jump off, then on two beer-barrels, and then on a painter's trestle about fifteen feet high. But it was no good. He could see he'd made a mistake.

'Now don't tell me,' I said, 'that this is all a mistake?'

No, he said. The idea of training a goat to fly was a mistake, that's all. Jethro could see that. No, what he did do was to breed a goat that could fly—you see how I mean, a sort of miracle. Jethro was a very religious chap—Salvation Army meetings, playing in the band, believing in the Bible and all that. And suddenly that's how he saw it. I want a flying goat, he thought, and if I want it badly enough and ask God then God will perform a miracle and see that I get it. If God doesn't approve I shan't get it and then I shall know it was wrong to ask for it. So he mated two of his goats and prayed for a miracle to happen and waited. He prayed twice a day, morning and night, for a kid that could fly. He knew all about miracles. If five thousand people could be fed with two loaves and five small fishes, or if somebody could raise a boy from the dead or if a sick man could pick up his bed and walk then why shouldn't an ordinary chap like himself get a simple thing like a goat that could fly? Ask yourself. It was reasonable.

'And now you're going to tell me,' I said, 'that in due course the kid was born and it could fly from birth like a bird?'

It was, he said, and it could. The second day of its life it began to jump up in the air. Like a lamb, only higher. Then the third it jumped higher still. The fourth day it flew over its mother. Flew, not jumped. Then by the end of the week it was flying over fences. It flew over a row of kidney-beans in Jethro's garden. Inside a month it could fly over a haystack. It was a lovely white colour, and Jethro told me it was so light that you could hold it in your hand like a ball of cotton wool.

'Then what?' I said.

Well, Jethro had another idea. It was through the Grace of God that I got the goat, he thought. The right thing to do is to devote it to the service of God in return. So he put it up to the Salvation Army—told them how God had wrought a miracle for him, tried to make them see how this flying goat was proof of the power of prayer, asked them to come and see it for themselves. Up to that time he'd kept it secret. Now he wanted all the world to know about it. Well, they were very sniffy, the Salvation Armyists. It looked like sacrilege. The power of prayer and miracle was kept for serious things—healing, faith, help in time of trouble, sin and sorrow and so on. A flying goat looked a bit like taking a rise out of the Almighty. Well, they argued and disagreed and then argued again, but at last Jethro persuaded them. The Salvation Armyists gathered in a field behind Jethro's house and waited for the goat to fly. It didn't do anything. It didn't even lift its feet off the ground. Well, just what we thought, they said, just what we expected. The man has not only made fools of us but has taken the name of God in vain. We'll see about this, and they did, to the extent that Jethro never set foot in the Salvation Army hall again and never played the euphonium for them any more.

'But still,' I said, 'the goat could fly?'

Yes, he said, the goat could fly. It flew better and better as it grew older and older. Jethro never trained it. Just fed it and it flew. The only thing Jethro used to do was whistle it home, and then when it came home it used to circle round and round like a homing pigeon. Well, soon after the Salvation Armyists turned him down Jethro had another idea. He decided to take the goat on tour. That's how he got in with the circus. At first, Jethro told me, they didn't believe him. Then when they saw that goat flying over a circus tent the circus folk went crazy. It was just the craziest thing ever seen in a circus. Better than man-eating lions, performing seals, dancing ponies and all that. Everybody had seen things like that, but nobody had ever seen a flying goat. It was a sensation. It went everywhere. Everywhere you went you saw the circus-bills about Jethro Watkins's flying goat.

'It's funny I never heard of it,' I said.

Funny, he said, I should think it is funny. Everybody's heard of Jethro Watkins's flying goat. Everybody.

'Except me,' I said. 'Well, what happened then?'

Well, Jethro thought he could do better for himself than the circus. So he struck out on his own. And that began the real sensational stuff. You know, flying off the top of the Tower at Blackpool and all that. You mean to say you never heard of that?

'No,' I said, 'I can't say I ever heard of it.'

It was in all the newspapers, he said. Pictures of it. Millions of people there. Don't you know what happened? A newspaper offered Jethro five thousand pounds if the goat would fly off the top of the Tower. Well, it flew off the top of the Tower and flew round over the sea for a few minutes and then settled on the pier. But that was nothing. You must have heard all about the time when it flew away from Belle Vue Manchester and was missing over the Pennines for a night and a day and then came flying home to Jethro's old home here as cool as you like? Why, he said, that was the biggest sensation of the lot.

'I bet it was,' I said. 'Now tell me it flew the Channel.'

Well, it did, he said, but that isn't what I was going to tell you about. I was going to tell you about the time it had kids.

'Don't tell me they could fly,' I said.

One could, he said, but not the other. That was funny, wasn't it? One kid was black, and one was white, and it was the white one that could fly. Jethro said it was marvellous. Better than the mother. The second day after it was born Jethro took it out and it flew round the church steeple. Well, if a goat could do that on the second day of its life, what was it going to do when it was a year old?

'You tell me,' I said. 'I don't know.'

Well, he said, that was the sad thing. Jethro died. He was always a fat chap and I think he must have got fatty heart or something.

Anyway the day he got the young goat to loop the loop the excitement must have been too much for him. He dropped down dead.

'The excitement,' I said, 'would have been too much for anybody. What happened to the goats after Jethro died?'

Well, he said, that's another funny thing. Nobody seems to know.

'They just flew away,' I said. 'Is that it?'

Well, nobody knows, he said. There were a lot of goats sold at auction after Jethro was dead, but none of them could fly.

'How many times did you see the flying goat?' I said. 'I mean you, yourself.'

Well, he said.

'Didn't you ever see it at all?'

Well, he said, to tell the truth I didn't. I heard all about it, but I never got the chance to see it.

'Didn't you ever know anybody who saw it?' I said.

No, he said, I can't say I did. Not exactly.

'Well,' I said, 'didn't you ever know anybody who knew anybody who'd seen it?'

No, he said, if it comes to that, I didn't. Not exactly.

'Then,' I said, 'tell me who told you all about it?'

Jethro, he said.

I didn't say anything this time.

Don't you believe it? he said.

'Oh! yes,' I said, 'I believe it.'

After all, he said, it takes no more believing than the feeding of five thousand people with two loaves and five small fishes, does it?

'Oh, no!' I said.

After all, he said, you can make yourself believe in anything if you want to, can't you?

'Oh! yes!' I said.

Well, he said, it's been very nice. I think I'll be getting along.

'No, you don't,' I said. 'Wait a minute. Just sit down. It's my turn to tell you something. I'd like to tell you about my uncle Walter's musical pig. Now when I was a boy my uncle Walter had a pig that played the trombone. I don't mean it was a pig that played the trombone with the trombone. I mean it was a pig that played the trombone without a trombone. Now this pig had a litter—'

Arnold Bennett

The Burglary

Lady Dain said: 'Jee, if that portrait stays there much longer, you'll
just have to take me off to Pirehill one of these fine mornings.'

Pirehill is the seat of the great local hospital; but it is also the
seat of the great local lunatic asylum; and when the inhabi-
tents of the Five Towns say merely 'Pirehill', they mean the
asylum.

'I do declare I can't fancy my food now-a-days,' said Lady Dain,
'and it's all that portrait!' She stared plaintively up at the immense
oil-painting which faced her as she sat at the breakfast-table in
her spacious and opulent dining-room.

Sir Jehoshaphat made no remark.

Despite Lady Dain's animadversions upon it, despite the un-
doubted fact that it was generally disliked in the Five Towns, the
portrait had cost a thousand pounds (some said guineas), and
though not yet two years old it was probably worth at least fifteen
hundred in the picture market. For it was a Cressage; and not
only was it a Cressage—it was one of the finest Cressages in
existence.

It marked the summit of Sir Jehoshaphat's career. Sir Jehoshaphat's career was, perhaps, the most successful and brilliant in the
entire social history of the Five Towns. This famous man was the
principal partner in Dain Brothers. His brother was dead, but two
of Sir Jee's sons were in the firm. Dain Brothers were the largest
manufacturers of cheap earthenware in the district, catering
chiefly for the American and Colonial buyer. They had an extremely bad reputation for cutting prices. They were hated by
every other firm in the Five Towns, and, to hear rival manufacturers talk, one would gather the impression that Sir Jee had
acquired a tremendous fortune by systematically selling goods
under cost. They were also hated by between eighteen and nine-
teen hundred employees. But such hatred, however virulent, had
not marred the progress of Sir Jee's career.

He had meant to make a name and he had made it. The Five
Towns might laugh at his vulgar snobbishness. The Five Towns

might sneer at his calculated philanthropy. But he was, nevertheless, the best-known man in the Five Towns, and it was precisely
his snobbishness and his philanthropy which had carried him to
the top. Moreover, he had been the first public man in the Five
Towns to gain a knighthood. The Five Towns could not deny that
it was very proud indeed of this knighthood. The means by which
he had won this distinction were neither here nor there—he had
won it. And was he not the father of his native borough? Had he
not been three times mayor of his native borough? Was not the
whole northern half of the county dotted and spangled by his bene-
factions, his institutions, his endowments?

And it could not be denied that he sometimes tickled the Five
Towns as the Five Towns likes being tickled. There was, for
example, the notorious Sneyd incident. Sneyd Hall, belonging to
the Earl of Chell, lies a few miles south of the Five Towns, and
from it the pretty Countess of Chell exercises that condescending
meddlesomeness which so frequently exasperates the Five Towns.
Sir Jee had got his title by the aid of the Countess—'Interfering
Iris', as she is locally dubbed. Shortly afterwards he had contrived
to quarrel with the Countess; and the quarrel was conducted by
Sir Jee as a quarrel between equals, which delighted the district.
Sir Jee's final word in it had been to buy a sizable tract of land
near Sneyd village, just off the Sneyd estate, and to erect thereon
a mansion quite as imposing as Sneyd Hall, and far more up to
date, and to call the mansion Sneyd Castle. A mighty stroke! Iris
was furious; the Earl speechless with fury. But they could do nothing. Naturally the Five Towns was tickled.

It was apropos of the house-warming of Sneyd Castle, also of
the completion of his third mayoralty, and of the inauguration of
the Dain Technical Institute, that the movement had been started
(primarily by a few toadies) for tendering to Sir Jee a popular gift
worthy to express the profound esteem in which he was officially
held in the Five Towns. It having been generally felt that the gift
should take the form of a portrait, a local dilettante had suggested
Cressage, and when the Five Towns had inquired into Cressage
and discovered that that genius from the United States was celebrated throughout the civilized world, and regarded as the equal
of Velazquez (whoever Velazquez might be), and that he had
painted half the aristocracy, and that his income was regal, the
suggestion was accepted and Cressage was approached.

Cressage haughtily consented to paint Sir Jee's portrait on his usual conditions; namely, that the sitter should go to the little village in Bedfordshire where Cressage had his principal studio, and that the painting should be exhibited at the Royal Academy before being shown anywhere else. (Cressage was an R.A., but no one thought of putting R.A. after his name. He was so big, that instead of the Royal Academy conferring distinction on him, he conferred distinction on the Royal Academy.)

Sir Jee went to Bedfordshire and was rapidly painted, and he came back gloomy. The presentation committee went to Bedfordshire later to inspect the portrait, and they, too, came back gloomy.

Then the Academy Exhibition opened, and the portrait, showing Sir Jee in his robe and chain and in a chair, was instantly hailed as possibly the most glorious masterpiece of modern times. All the critics were of one accord. The committee and Sir Jee were reassured, but only partially, and Sir Jee rather less so than the committee. For there was something in the enthusiastic criticism which gravely disturbed him. An enlightened generation, thoroughly familiar with the dazzling yearly succession of Cressage's portraits, need not be told what this something was. One critic wrote that Cressage displayed even more than his 'customary astounding insight into character ...' Another critic wrote that Cressage's observation was, as usual, 'calmly and coldly hostile'. Another referred to the 'typical provincial mayor, immortalized for the diversion of future ages'.

Inhabitants of the Five Towns went to London to see the work for which they had subscribed, and they saw a mean, little, old man, with thin lips and a straggling grey beard, and shifty eyes, and pushful snob written all over him; ridiculous in his gewgaws of office. When you looked at the picture close to, it was a meaningless mass of coloured smudges, but when you stood fifteen feet away from it the portrait was absolutely life-like, amazing, miraculous. It was so wondrously life-like that some of the inhabitants of the Five Towns burst out laughing. Many people felt sorry—not for Sir Jee—but for Lady Dain. Lady Dain was beloved and genuinely respected. She was a simple, homely, sincere woman, her one weakness being that she had never been able to see through Sir Jee.

Of course, at the presentation ceremony the portrait had been ecstatically referred to as a possession precious for ever, and the recipient and his wife pretended to be overflowing with pure joy in the ownership of it.

It had been hanging in the dining-room of Sneyd Castle about sixteen months, when Lady Dain told her husband that it would ultimately drive her into the lunatic asylum.

'Don't be silly, wife,' said Sir Jee. 'I wouldn't part with that portrait for ten times what it cost.'

This was, to speak bluntly, a downright lie. Sir Jee secretly hated the portrait more than anyone hated it. He would have been almost ready to burn down Sneyd Castle in order to get rid of the thing. But it happened that on the previous evening, in the conversation with the magistrates' clerk, his receptive brain had been visited by a less expensive scheme than burning down the castle.

Lady Dain sighed.

'Are you going to town early?' she inquired.

'Yes,' he replied. 'I'm on the rota today.'

He was chairman of the borough bench of magistrates. As he drove into town he revolved his scheme and thought it wild and dangerous, but still feasible.

On the Bench that morning Sir Jee shocked Mr Sherratt, the magistrates' clerk, and he utterly disgusted Mr Bourne, superintendent of the borough police. (I do not intend to name the name of the borough—whether Bursley, Hanbridge, Knype, Longshaw, or Turnhill. The inhabitants of the Five Towns will know without being told; the rest of the world has no right to know.) There had recently occurred a somewhat thrilling series of burglaries in the district, and the burglars (a gang of them was presumed) had escaped the solicitous attentions of the police. But on the previous afternoon an underling of Mr Bourne's had caught a man who was generally believed to be wholly or partly responsible for the burglaries. The Five Towns breathed with relief and congratulated Mr Bourne; and Mr Bourne was well pleased with himself. The *Staffordshire Signal* headed the item of news, 'Smart Capture of a Supposed Burglar'. The supposed burglar gave his name as William Smith, and otherwise behaved in an extremely suspicious manner.

Now, Sir Jee, sitting as chief magistrate in the police-court, actually dismissed the charge against the man! Overruling his sole colleague on the Bench that morning, Alderman Easton, he dismissed the charge against William Smith, holding that the evidence for the prosecution was insufficient to justify even a remand. No wonder that Mr Bourne was discouraged, not to say angry. No wonder that that pillar of the law, Mr Sherratt, was pained and shocked. At the conclusion of the case Sir Jehoshaphat said that he would be glad to speak with William Smith afterwards in the magistrates' room, indicating that he sympathized with William Smith, and wished to exercise upon William Smith his renowned philanthropy.

And so, at about noon, when the Court majestically rose, Sir Jee retired to the magistrates' room, where the humble Alderman Easton was discreet enough not to follow him, and awaited William Smith. And William Smith came, guided thither by a policeman, to whom, in parting from him, he made a rude surreptitious gesture.

Sir Jee, seated in the arm-chair which dominates the other chairs round the elm table in the magistrates' room, emitted a preliminary cough.

'Smith,' he said sternly, leaning his elbows on the table, 'you were very fortunate this morning, you know.'

And he gazed at Smith.

Smith stood near the door, cap in hand. He did not resemble a burglar, who surely ought to be big, muscular, and masterful. He resembled an undersized clerk who has been out of work for a long time, but who has nevertheless found the means to eat and drink rather plenteously. He was clothed in a very shabby navy-blue suit, frayed at the wrists and ankles, and greasy in front. His linen collar was brown with dirt, his fingers were dirty, his hair was unkempt and long, and a young and lusty black beard was sprouting on his chin. His boots were not at all pleasant.

'Yes, governor,' Smith replied, lightly, with a Manchester accent. 'And what's *your* game?'

Sir Jee was taken aback. He, the chairman of the borough Bench, and the leading philanthropist in the country, to be so spoken to! But what could he do? He himself had legally established Smith's innocence. Smith was as free as air, and had a perfect right to adopt any tone he chose to any man he chose. And Sir Jee desired a service from William Smith.

'I was hoping I might be of use to you,' said Sir Jehoshaphat diplomatically.

'Well,' said Smith, 'that's all right, that is. But none of your philanthropic dodges, you know. I don't want to lead a new life, and I don't want to turn over a new leaf, and I don't want a helpin' hand, nor none o' those things. And, what's more, I don't want a situation. I've got all the situation as I need. But I never refuse money, nor beer neither. Never did, and I'm forty years old next month.'

'I suppose burgling doesn't pay very well, does it?' Sir Jee boldly ventured.

William Smith laughed coarsely.

'It pays right enough,' said he. 'But I don't put my money on my back, governor, I put it into a bit of public-house property when I get the chance.'

'It may pay,' said Sir Jee. 'But it is wrong. It is very anti-social.'

'Is it, indeed?' Smith returned dryly. 'Anti-social, is it? Well, I've heard it called plenty o' things in my time, but never that. Now, I should have called it quite sociablelike, sort of making free with strangers, and so on. However,' he added, 'I come across a cove once as told me crime was nothing but a disease and ought to be treated as such. I asked him for a dozen o' port, but he never sent it.'

'Ever been caught before?' Sir Jee inquired.

'Not much!' Smith exclaimed. 'And this'll be a lesson to me, I can tell you. Now, what are you getting at, governor? Because my time's money, my time is.'

Sir Jee coughed once more.

'Sit down,' said Sir Jee.

And William Smith sat down opposite to him at the table, and put his shiny elbows on the table precisely in the manner of Sir Jee's elbows.

'Well?' he cheerfully encouraged Sir Jee.

'How would you like to commit a burglary that was not a crime?' said Sir Jee, his shifty eyes wandering around the room. 'A perfectly lawful burglary?'

'What are you getting at?' William Smith was genuinely astonished.

'At my residence, Sneyd Castle,' Sir Jee proceeded, 'there's a large portrait of myself in the dining-room that I want to have stolen. You understand?'

'Stolen?'

'Yes. I want to get rid of it. And I want—er—people to think that it has been stolen.'

'Well, why don't you stop up one night and steal it yourself, and then burn it?' William Smith suggested.

'That would be deceitful,' said Sir Jee, gravely. 'I could not tell my friends that the portrait had been stolen if it had not been stolen. The burglary must be entirely genuine.'

'What's the figure?' said Smith curtly.

'Figure?'

'What are you going to give me for the job?'

'Give you for doing the job?' Sir Jee repeated, his secret and ineradicable meanness aroused. 'Give you? Why, I'm giving you the opportunity to honestly steal a picture that's worth over a thousand pounds—I dare say it would be worth two thousand pounds in America—and you want to be paid into the bargain! Do you know, my man, that people come all the way from Manchester, and even London, to see that portrait?' He told Smith about the painting.

'Then why are you in such a stew to be rid of it?' queried the burglar.

'That's my affair,' said Sir Jee. 'I don't like it. Lady Dain doesn't like it. But it's a presentation portrait, and so I can't—you see, Mr Smith?'

'And how am I going to dispose of it when I've got it?' Smith demanded. 'You can't melt a portrait down as if it was silver. By what you say, governor, it's known all over the blessed world. Seems to me I might just as well try to sell the Nelson Column.'

'Oh, nonsense!' said Sir Jee. 'Nonsense. You'll sell it in America quite easily. It'll be a fortune to you. Keep it for a year first, and then send it to New York.'

William Smith shook his head and drummed his fingers on the table; and then quite suddenly he brightened and said—

'All right, governor. I'll take it on, just to oblige you.'

'When can you do it?' asked Sir Jee, hardly concealing his joy. 'Tonight?'

'No,' said Smith, mysteriously. 'I'm engaged tonight.'

'Well, tomorrow night?'

'Nor tomorrow. I'm engaged tomorrow too.'

'You seem to be very much engaged, my man,' Sir Jee observed.

'What do you expect?' Smith retorted. 'Business is business. I could do it the night after tomorrow.'

'But that's Christmas Eve,' Sir Jee protested.

'What if it is Christmas Eve?' said Smith coldly. 'Would you prefer Christmas Day? I'm engaged on Boxing Day and the day after.'

'Not in the Five Towns, I trust?' Sir Jee remarked.

'No,' said Smith shortly. 'The Five Towns is about sucked dry.'

The affair was arranged for Christmas Eve.

'Now,' Sir Jee suggested, 'shall I draw you a plan of the castle, so that you can—'

William Smith's face expressed terrific scorn. 'Do you suppose,' he said, 'as I haven't had plans o' your castle ever since it was built? What do you take me for? I'm not a blooming excursionist, I'm not. I'm a business man— that's what I am.'

Sir Jee was snubbed, and he agreed submissively to all William Smith's arrangements for the innocent burglary. He perceived that in William Smith he had stumbled on a professional of the highest class, and this good fortune pleased him.

'There's only one thing that riles me,' said Smith, in parting, 'and that is that you'll go and say that after you'd done everything you could for me I went and burgled your castle. And you'll talk about the ingratitude of the lower classes. I know you, governor!'

On the afternoon of the 24th of December Sir Jehoshaphat drove home to Sneyd Castle from the principal of the three Dain manufactories, and found Lady Dain superintending the work of packing up trunks. He and she were to quit the castle that afternoon in order to spend Christmas on the other side of the Five Towns, under the roof of their eldest son, John, who had a new house, a new wife, and a new baby (male). John was a domineering person, and, being rather proud of his house and all that was his, he had obstinately decided to have his own Christmas at his own hearth. Grandpapa and Grandmamma, drawn by the irresistible attraction of that novelty, a grandson (though Mrs John had declined to have the little thing named Jehoshaphat), had yielded to John's solicitations, and the family gathering, for the first time in history, was not to occur round Sir Jee's mahogany.

Sir Jee, very characteristically, said nothing to Lady Dain immediately. He allowed her to proceed with the packing of the trunks, and then tea was served, and as the time was approaching for the carriage to come round to take them to the station, at last he suddenly remarked—

'I shan't be able to go with you to John's this afternoon.'

'Oh, Jee!' she exclaimed. 'Really, you are tiresome. Why couldn't you tell me before?'

'I will come over tomorrow morning—perhaps in time for church,' he proceeded, ignoring her demand for an explanation.

He always did ignore her demand for an explanation. Indeed, she only asked for explanations in a mechanical and perfunctory manner—she had long since ceased to expect them. Sir Jee had been born like that—devious, mysterious, incalculable. And Lady Dain accepted him as he was. She was somewhat surprised, therefore, when he went on—

'I have some minutes of committee meetings that I really must go carefully through and send off tonight, and you know as well as I do that there'll be no chance of doing that at John's. I've telegraphed to John.'

He was obviously nervous and self-conscious.

'There's no food in the house,' sighed Lady Dain. 'And the servants are all going away except Callear, and he can't cook your dinner tonight. I think I'd better stay myself and look after you.'

'You'll do no such thing,' said Sir Jee, decisively. 'As for my dinner, anything will do for that. The servants have been promised their holiday, to start from this evening, and they must have it. I can manage.'

Here spoke the philanthropist with his unshakable sense of justice.

So Lady Dain departed, anxious and worried, having previously arranged something cold for Sir Jee in the dining-room, and instructed Callear about boiling the water for Sir Jee's tea on Christmas morning. Callear was the under-coachman and a useful old man. He it was who would drive Sir Jee to the station on Christmas morning, and then guard the castle and the stables thereof during the absence of the family and the other servants. Callear slept over the stables.

And after Sir Jee had consumed his cold repast in the dining-room the other servants went, and Sir Jee was alone in the castle, facing the portrait.

He had managed the affair fairly well, he thought. Indeed, he had a talent for chicane, and none knew it better than himself. It would have been dangerous if the servants had been left in the castle. They might have suffered from insomnia, and heard William Smith, and interfered with the operations of William Smith. On the other hand, Sir Jee had no intention whatever of leaving the castle uninhabited to the mercies of William Smith. He felt that he himself must be on the spot to see that everything went right and that nothing went wrong. Thus, the previously-arranged scheme for the servants' holiday fitted perfectly into his plans, and all that he had had to do was to refuse to leave the castle till the morrow. It was ideal.

Nevertheless, he was a little afraid of what he had done, and of what he was going to permit William Smith to do. It was certainly dangerous—certainly rather a wild scheme. However, the die was cast. And within twelve hours he would be relieved of the intolerable incubus of the portrait.

And when he thought of the humiliations which that portrait had caused him; when he remembered the remarks of his sons concerning it, especially John's remarks; when he recalled phrases about it in London newspapers, he squirmed, and told himself that no scheme for getting rid of it could be too wild and perilous. And, after all, the burglary dodge was the only dodge, absolutely the only conceivable practical method of disposing of the portrait—except burning down the castle. And surely it was preferable to a conflagration, to arson! Moreover, in case of fire at the castle some blundering fool would be sure to cry: 'The portrait! The portrait must be saved!' And the portrait would be saved.

He gazed at the repulsive, hateful thing. In the centre of the lower part of the massive gold frame was the legend: 'Presented to Sir Jehoshaphat Dain, Knight, as a mark of public esteem and gratitude', etc. He wondered if William Smith would steal the frame. It was to be hoped that he would not steal the frame. In fact, William Smith would find it very difficult to steal that frame unless he had an accomplice or so.

'This is the last time I shall see you!' said Sir Jee to the portrait.

Then he unfastened the catch of one of the windows in the dining-room (as per contract with William Smith), turned out the electric light, and went to bed in the deserted castle.

He went to bed, but not to sleep. It was no part of Sir Jee's programme to sleep. He intended to listen, and he did listen.

And about two o'clock, precisely the hour which William Smith had indicated, he fancied he heard muffled and discreet noises. Then he was sure that he heard them. William Smith had kept his word. Then the noises ceased for a period, and then they recommenced. Sir Jee restrained his curiosity as long as he could, and when he could restrain it no more he rose and silently opened his bedroom window and put his head out into the nipping night air of Christmas. And by good fortune he saw the vast oblong of the picture, carefully enveloped in sheets, being passed by a couple of dark figures through the dining-room window to the garden outside. William Smith had a colleague, then, and he was taking the frame as well as the canvas. Sir Jee watched the men disappear down the avenue, and they did not reappear. Sir Jee returned to bed.

Yes, he felt himself equal to facing it out with his family and friends. He felt himself equal to pretending that he had no knowledge of the burglary.

Having slept a few hours, he got up early and, half-dressed, descended to the dining-room just to see what sort of a mess William Smith had made.

The canvas of the portrait lay flat on the hearthrug, with the following words written on it in chalk: 'This is no use to me.' It was the massive gold frame that had gone.

Further, as was later discovered, all the silver had gone. Not a spoon was left in the castle.

John Collier

Rope Enough

Henry Fraser, well assured that almost everything is done by mirrors, was given a job in India. No sooner had he set foot on shore than he burst into a horse-laugh. Those who were meeting him asked in some alarm the cause of this merriment. He replied he was laughing at the mere idea of the Indian Rope Trick.

He emitted similar startling sounds, and gave the same explanation, at a tiffin where he was officially made welcome; likewise on the Maidan, over *chota peg*, in rickshaws, in bazaars, in the Club, and on the polo ground. Soon he was known from Bombay to Calcutta as the man who laughed at the Indian Rope Trick, and he gloried in the well-deserved publicity.

There came a day, however, when he was sitting in his bungalow, bored to death. His boy entered, and, with suitable salaams, announced that a mountebank was outside, who craved the honour of entertaining the sahib with a performance of the Indian Rope Trick. Laughing heartily, Henry consented, and moved out to his chair upon the veranda.

Below, in the dusty compound, stood a native who was emaciated to a degree, and who had with him a spry youngster, a huge mat basket, and a monstrous great sword. Out of the basket he dragged some thirty feet of stout rope, made a pass or two, and slung it up into the air. It stayed there. Henry chuckled.

The boy then, with a caper, sprang at the rope, clutched it, and went up hand over hand, like a monkey. When he reached the top he vanished into thin air. Henry guffawed.

Soon the man, looking upwards with an anxious expression, began to hoot and holler after the boy. He called him down, he ordered him down, he begged him down, he began to swear and curse horribly. The boy, it seemed, took no notice at all. Henry roared.

Now the black, clapping his abominable great scimitar between his teeth, took hold of the rope himself, and went up it like a sailor. He, also, disappeared at the top. Henry's mirth increased.

Pretty soon some yelps and squeals were heard coming out of

the empty air, and then a blood-curdling scream. Down came
a leg, thump on to the ground, then an arm, a thigh, a head
and other joints, and finally (no ladies being present) a bare back-
side, which struck the earth like a bomb. Henry went into
fits.

Then the black came sliding down, holding on with one hand,
fairly gibbering with excitement. He presented to Henry, with a
salaam, his reeking blade for inspection. Henry rocked in his chair.

The black, seemingly overwhelmed with remorse, gathered up
the fragments of his little stooge, lavishing a hundred lamentations
and endearments upon each grisly member, and he stowed them
all in the giant basket.

At that moment Henry, feeling the time had come for a show-
down, and willing to bet a thousand to one they'd planted the
whole compound full of mirrors before calling him out there, pulled
out his revolver, and blazed away all six chambers in different
directions, in the expectation of splintering at least one of those
deceiving glasses.

Nothing of that sort happened, but the black, doing a quick
pirouette in alarm, looked down in the dust at his feet, and held
up a villainous little snake, no thicker than a lead pencil, which
had been killed by one of Henry's stray bullets. He gave a gasp
of relief, touched his turban very civilly, turned round again, and
made a pass or two over the basket. At once, with a wriggle and
a frisk, the boy sprang out, whole, alive, smiling, full of health and
wickedness.

The black hastily hauled down the rope, and came cringing up
to Henry, overflowing with gratitude for having been saved from
the villainous little snake, which was nothing more nor less than
a krait—one nip and a man goes round and round like a Catherine
wheel for eleven seconds; then he is as dead as mutton.

'But for the Heavenborn,' said the black, 'I should have been
a goner, and my wicked little boy here, who is my pride and
delight, must have lain dismembered in the basket till the sahib's
servants condescended to throw him to the crocodiles. Our worth-
less lives, our scanty goods, are all at the sahib's disposal.'

'That's all right,' said Henry. 'All I ask is, show me how the
trick is worked, or the laugh will be on me from now on.'

'Would not the sahib,' said the black diffidently, 'prefer the
secret of a superb hair-restorer?'

'No. No,' said Henry. 'Nothing but the trick.'

'I have,' said the black, 'the secret of a very peculiar tonic, which the sahib (not now, of course, but in later life) might find—'

'The trick,' said Henry, 'and without further delay.'

'Very well,' said the black. 'Nothing in the world could be more simple. You make a pass, like that—'

'Wait a minute,' said Henry. 'Like that?'

'Exactly,' said the black. 'You then throw up the rope—so. You see? It sticks.'

'So it does,' said Henry.

'Any boy can climb,' said the black. 'Up, boy! Show the sahib.'

The boy, smiling, climbed up and disappeared.

'Now,' said the black, 'if the sahib will excuse me, I shall be back immediately.' And with that he climbed up himself, threw down the boy in sections, and speedily rejoined Henry on the ground.

'All that,' said he, scooping up legs and arms as he spoke, 'all that can be done by anyone. There is a little knack, however, to the pass I make at this juncture. If the sahib will deign to observe closely—like that.'

'Like that?' said Henry.

'You have it to perfection,' said the black.

'Very interesting,' said Henry. 'Tell me, what's up there at the top of the rope?'

'Ah, sahib,' said the black with a smile, 'that is something truly delightful.'

With that he salaamed and departed, taking with him his rope, his giant basket, his tremendous great scimitar, and his wicked little boy. Henry was left feeling rather morose: he was known from the Deccan to the Khyber Pass as the man who laughed at the Indian Rope Trick, and now he could laugh no more.

He decided to keep very quiet about it, but this unfortunately was not enough. At tiffin, at *chota peg*, at the Club, on the Maidan, in the bazaar, and at polo, he was expected to laugh like a horse, and in India one has to do what is expected of one. Henry became extremely unpopular, cabals were formed against him, and soon he was hoofed out of the Service.

This was the more distressing as in the meantime he had married a wife, strong-featured, upstanding, well groomed, straight-eyed, a little peremptory in manner, and as jealous as a demon, but in all respects a memsahib of the highest type, who knew very well what was due to her. She told Henry he had better go to America and make a fortune. He agreed, they packed up, and off they went to America.

'I hope,' said Henry, as they stood looking at the sky-line of New York, 'I hope I shall make that fortune.'

'Of course,' said she. 'You must insist upon it.'

'Very well, my dear,' said he.

On landing, however, he discovered that all the fortunes had already been made, a discovery which very generally awaits those who visit America on this errand, and after some weeks of drifting about from place to place, he was prepared to cut his demand down to a mere job, then to a lesser job, and finally to the price of a meal and a bed for the night.

They reached this extremity in a certain small town in the Middle West. 'There is nothing for it, my dear,' said Henry. 'We shall have to do the Indian Rope Trick.'

His wife cried out very bitterly at the idea of a memsahib performing this native feat in a Middle Western town, before a Middle Western audience. She reproached him with the loss of his job, the poor quality of his manhood, with the time he let her little dog get run over on the bund, and with a glance he had cast at a Parsee maiden at Bombay. Nevertheless, reason and hunger prevailed: they pawned her last trinket, and invested in a rope, a roomy grip, and a monstrous old rusty scimitar they discovered in a junk-shop.

When she saw this last, Henry's wife flatly refused to go on, unless she was given the star part and Henry took that of the stooge. 'But,' said Henry, drawing an apprehensive thumb down the notched and jagged edge of the grim and rusty bilbo—'But,' said he, 'you don't know how to make the passes.'

'You shall teach me,' she said, 'and if anything goes wrong you will have only yourself to blame.'

So Henry showed her. You may be sure he was very thorough in his instructions. In the end she mastered them perfectly, and there was nothing left to do but to stain themselves with coffee. Henry improvised a turban and loin-cloth: she wore a *sari* and a pair of ash-trays borrowed from the hotel. They sought out a convenient waste lot, a large crowd collected, and the show began.

Up went the rope. Sure enough, it stuck. The crowd, with a multiple snigger, whispered that everything was done by mirrors. Henry, not without a good deal of puffing, went up hand over hand. When he got to the top, he forgot the crowd, the act, his wife, and even himself, so surprised and delighted was he by the sight that met his eyes.

He found himself crawling out of something like a well, on to what seemed to be solid ground. The landscape about him was not at all like that below: it was like an Indian paradise, full of dells, bowers, scarlet ibises, and heaven knows what all. However, his surprise and delight came less from these features of the background than from the presence of a young female in the nearest of these bowers or arbours, which happened to be all wreathed, canopied, overgrown and intertwined with passion flowers. This delightful creature, who was a positive houri, and very lightly attired, seemed to be expecting Henry, and greeted him with rapture.

Henry, who had a sufficiently affectionate nature, flung his arms round her neck and gazed deeply into her eyes. These were surprisingly eloquent: they seemed to say, 'Why not make hey hey while the sun shines?'

He found the notion entirely agreeable, and planted a lingering kiss on her lips, noting only with a dim and careless annoyance that his wife was hooting and hollering from below. 'What person of any tact or delicacy,' thought he, 'could hoot and holler at such a moment?' and he dismissed her from his mind.

You may imagine his mortification when his delicious damsel suddenly repulsed him from her arms. He looked over his shoulder, and there was his wife, clambering over the edge, terribly red in the face, with the fury of a demon in her eye, and the mighty scimitar gripped well between her teeth.

Henry tried to rise, but she was beforehand with him, and while yet he had but one foot on the ground, she caught him one across the loins with the huge and jagged bilbo, which effectually hamstrung him, so that he fell grovelling at her feet. 'For heaven's sake!' he cried. 'It's all a trick. Part of the act. It means nothing. Remember our public. The show must go on.'

'It shall,' said she, striking at his arms and legs.

'Oh, those notches!' cried he. 'I beg you, my dear, sharpen it a little upon a stone.'

'It is good enough for you, you viper,' said she, hacking away all the time. Pretty soon Henry was a limbless trunk.

'For the love of God,' said he, 'I hope you remember the passes. I can explain everything.'

'To hell with the passes!' said she, and with a last swipe she sent his head rolling like a football.

She was not long in picking up the scattered fragments of poor Henry, and flinging them down to earth, amid the applause and laughter of the crowd, who were more than ever convinced it was all done by mirrors.

Then, gripping her scimitar, she was about to swarm down after him, not from any soft-hearted intention of reassembling her unfortunate spouse, but rather to have another hack or two at some of the larger joints. At that moment she became aware of someone behind her, and, looking round, there was a divine young man, with the appearance of a Maharaja of the highest caste, an absolute Valentino, in whose eyes she seemed to read the words, 'It is better to burn upon the bed of passion than in the chair of electricity.'

This idea presented itself with an overwhelming appeal. She paused only to thrust her head through the aperture, and cry, 'That's what happens to a pig of a man who betrays his wife with a beastly native,' before hauling up the rope and entering into conversation with her charmer.

The police soon appeared upon the scene. There was nothing but a cooing sound above, as if invisible turtle doves were circling in amorous flight. Below, the various portions of Henry were scattered in the dust, and the blue-bottle flies were already settling upon them.

The crowd explained it was nothing but a trick, done with mirrors.

'It looks to me,' said the sergeant, 'as if the biggest one must have splintered right on top of him.'

Alan Coren

On a Wing and a Prayer

'*The largest known creature ever to have flown, an extinct reptile with an estimated wingspan of fifty-one feet, has been discovered by fossil hunters in West Texas. The creature had twice the wingspan of the biggest previously known pterodactyl.*' The Times

From a hole in a rock just outside what was to become Sevenoaks, Homo Britannicus slowly emerged into the grey morning. A single snowflake floated down and settled on his forearm, paused, and dissolved among the thick, matted hair. He watched it disappear, his thin rim of forehead wrinkling.

A second landed on his broad flat nose. He squinted at it until it became a droplet, and until that droplet vanished.

'What's it like out?' called his wife, from the dark recess of the cave. H. Britannicus shivered.

'Bloody freezing,' he said. 'Also, promise you won't laugh, the rain is coming down in bits.'

His wife scuttled out, her lovely knuckles skimming the ground.

'What?' she said.

'Look,' he said. 'Bits.'

She looked at the snow, and she looked at the leaden sky.

'That'll be the Ice Age coming, then,' she said.

'Here,' said H. Britannicus, 'what's that grey coming out of your mouth?'

'It's coming out of yours as well,' she snapped. 'How do I know what it is, I've never been in an Ice Age before, have I?'

H. Britannicus shook his head slowly. Tiny Pleistocene items flew out of his thatch, and hitting the chilly air, immediately became extinct.

'What's it all coming to?' said H. Britannicus. 'Where will it all end? When I was a kid, the summers we had!'

'I blame,' said his wife, 'the tool. All these bone needles, all these flint hammers, it's not natural.'

'Progress,' said her husband. 'You got to have progress.'

He tried to stand a little more erect. It wasn't easy. 'I'm off for a bit of a stroll,' he said. 'I'll catch me death standing here.'

It was just outside what is now the sub-soil of Canterbury that Homo Britannicus glanced up through his rime-hung eye-brows and noticed a figure shambling towards him. It had a pterodactyl on its arm.

'Morning,' said Homo Britannicus, taking a firmer grip on his club, just in case.

'Bonjour,' said the figure.

H. Britannicus raised his club slightly.

'What?' he said.

'Mah nem,' said the figure, 'eez Omo Gallicus. 'Ow eez eet going?'

'Mustn't grumble,' said Homo Britannicus. 'Where are you from?'

Homo Gallicus pointed behind him with his free hand, towards France.

'Ah 'ave walk many days,' said Homo Gallicus, 'wiz a proposition.'

'It looks like an ordinary bloody pterodactyl to me,' said Homo Britannicus. 'And what's that round your neck?'

'Wi call zem onions,' said Homo Gallicus.

Homo Britannicus reached out and felt one, cautiously.

'You'll never kill nothing with that, son,' he said. 'Too soft.'

'Wi eat zem,' said Homo Gallicus.

Homo Britannicus looked at him.

'It takes all sorts,' he said. 'What's the pterodactyl for?'

'Where can wi talk?' replied Homo Gallicus.

They found a small cave, and crept inside, and sat down. Homo Britannicus blew on his fingers.

'I wish we had a couple of sticks,' he said.

'What for?'

Homo Britannicus thought for a while.

'I'm not sure,' he said, at last. He nodded towards the pterodactyl. 'What about him, then?'

'In mah country,' began Homo Gallicus, 'wi 'ave no dinosaurs. Zer dinosaur eez—'ow you say?'

'Extinct.'

'Exactement! 'Owevaire, wi 'ave zer pterodactyl. You, on zer uzzer 'and, 'ave no pterodactyl, but you 'ave zer dinosaur, n'est-ce pas?'

'Just a few,' said Homo Britannicus. 'They're a bit bloody ropey, mind. Past their best, know what I mean? We've let 'em run down, werl, there's no call for 'em these days, is there?'

'Ah beg to diffaire,' said Homo Gallicus. He bent forward and his black eyes glittered. 'Mah plan eez to mate zer Gallic pterodactyl wiz zer Britannic dinosaur! Wi will produce zer Gallo-Britannic pterosaur, mon vieux! Eet weel be zer biggest flying objeck evaire seen!'

'So what?'

'Zer Ice Age is coming, hein?' said Homo Gallicus. 'In an eon or two, eet weel be 'ere. Wi weel 'ave to find warmaire climate, or . . .' he drew a thick finger across his imperceptible neck. 'Wi cannot walk, eet eez too far; so wi weel climb aboard zer giant pterosaur—*an' wi weel fly there!*'

'Gerroff!' cried Homo Britannicus.

'Also,' continued Homo Gallicus, unruffled, 'wi weel rule zer worl'! Everyone weel want one. Wi weel clean up zer pterosaur market.'

Homo Britannicus, to be fair, did all he could to fathom this momentous idea: he furrowed his millimetric brow, he scratched his craggy head, he sucked his great green teeth. But it was not until Homo Gallicus began to draw upon the cave-wall with his easy, flowing line, that his partner-to-be was really convinced.

It looked wonderful, in the picture.

Over the next five years, the innumerable, unforeseeable technological problems came forth and multiplied.

For two years alone, the dinosaur and the pterodactyl could not be persuaded to mate at all, and the wretched co-partners were forced to stand by while the two halves of the project shrieked and bit one another. But in the third year, by a process of strategic starving, feeding, and cajoling, the message got gradually through, and the dinosaur fell pregnant, ultimately giving birth to an enormous saurian cylinder with six legs and two very small wings. It flapped these latter for a few impotent beats, fell over, and expired.

'Ah well,' said Homo Gallicus, 'back to zer cave-wall!'

Which was all very well, except that the family of Homo Britannicus was finding it more and more difficult to make ends meet:

it was not merely that most of their breadwinner's time was spent in husbanding the animals involved, but also that those animals were consuming a vast amount of food. They were being saved from natural extinction only at the expense of the unfortunate hominids who had been forced to cast their lot with them.

'You never told us it would cost this much,' was how Homo Britannicus's wife put it, over and over agin.

Whereupon her husband would flatten her with his club, a gesture which over the years was becoming less and less affectionate.

But towards the end of the fifth year (by which time the temperature had dropped to a constant ten below zero, and the emaciated families of the luckless inventors reduced to gnawing for nourishment upon the misshapen bones of past failed experiments), a small pterosaur was produced of rather pleasing proportions. Even more encouraging was the fact that when it flapped its large leathery wings, it actually took off, flew for a few yards, and landed again without breaking anything.

'It works!' shrieked the two Homos, hugging one another and dancing great whorls in the encircling snow. 'A new dawn is breaking!'

'Erk,' went the baby pterosaur. It opened its mouth wide, 'Erk.'

'Eet wants,' said Homo Gallicus, 'to be fed.'

For five more years they fed it, while it grew bigger and bigger. The cold wind that continued to blow through Europe having taken its constant toll, the vegetation was now so sparse that the family of Homo Britannicus spent its every waking hour in scouring the white landscape for pterosaur fodder, they themselves subsisting on grubs and bits of bark and anything else the pterosaur could not use.

'When will it be big enough?' they would plead of the manufacturers, 'when will it be ready? When will it all end? When will the miracle begin?'

And the manufacturers, by now mere hirsute skeletons themselves, would say: 'Soon, soon.'

And then, in the bleak autumn of the tenth year, when its wingspan had reached fifty-one feet, and its sleek giant body was consuming a field a day, and its insistent 'ERK! ERK!' had reached a pitch and volume that would start avalanches rolling a dozen leagues away, they trundled the Gallo-Britannic pterosaur out of its enormous cave, and announced that it was ready.

'Wi weel head West,' cried Homo Gallicus, 'to zer sun and zer fleshpots.'

Homo Britannicus clubbed his wife for the last time, tenderly.

'Back in two shakes,' he said, and gathering the mangy ratskins about his jutting bones, he and his colleague climbed aboard.

The great wings flapped, and the pterosaur lumbered down the runway in a trail of webby pot-holes, and took off.

The last thing they saw, before the freezing snow-clouds enfolded them, was the pitiful little knot of rags beneath, staring upwards.

They seemed to be praying.

It was warm in the place that was subsequently Dallas.

A group of fat, balding hominids were sitting around a tri-ceratops-shaped pool, examining a roughly circular rock that Homo Texus was rolling up and down.

'I agree,' said Homo Oklahomus, who had made the trip especially to see it, 'it could be very big. It could be, like, very big indeed.'

'With the right packaging,' said Homo Arkansus.

'With the right packaging,' said Homo Oklahomus, nodding.

It was at that point that the sun was blotted out.

'What the—!' cried Homo Texus, letting the wheel roll from his fingers.

They leapt up, as the pterosaur came in to a perfect two-point landing, and ran across. Homos Gallicus and Britannicus jumped down.

'This is private property, buddy!' shouted Homo Texus.

'And this,' cried Homo Britannicus, 'is the Gallo-Britannic pterosaur! It will revolutionize travel, it will open up whole new experiences, it will ...'

'The hell it will!' shrieked Homo Texus.

'Did you hear the goddam noise?' screamed Homo Oklahomus.

'My God!' yelled Homo Arkansus, pointing a trembling finger, 'look at its damn droppings!'

'The environment!' howled the Americans. 'The environment!'

Whereupon, brushing aside the enfeebled European bonebags, they fell upon the hapless pterosaur, and beat it to death.

Thomas Hardy

Tony Kytes, the Arch-Deceiver

'I shall never forget Tony's face. 'Twas a little, round, firm, tight face, with a seam here and there left by the smallpox, but not enough to hurt his looks in a woman's eye, though he'd had it badish when he was a boy. So very serious looking and unsmiling 'a was, that young man, that it really seemed as if he couldn't laugh at all without great pain to his conscience. He looked very hard at a small speck in your eye when talking to 'ee. And there was no more sign of a whisker or beard on Tony Kytes's face than on the palm of my hand. He used to sing "The Tailor's Breeches" with a religious manner, as if it were a hymn:

'"*O the petticoats went off, and the breeches they went on!*"

and all the rest of the scandalous stuff. He was quite the women's favourite, and in return for their likings he loved 'em in shoals.

'But in course of time Tony got fixed down to one in particular, Milly Richards, a nice, light, small, tender little thing; and it was soon said that they were engaged to be married. One Saturday he had been to market to do business for his father, and was driving home the waggon in the afternoon. When he reached the foot of the very hill we shall be going over in ten minutes who should he see waiting for him at the top but Unity Sallet, a handsome girl, one of the young women he'd been very tender toward before he'd got engaged to Milly.

'As soon as Tony came up to her she said, "My dear Tony, will you give me a lift home?"

'"That I will, darling," said Tony. "You don't suppose I could refuse 'ee?"

'She smiled a smile, and up she hopped, and on drove Tony.

'"Tony," she says, in a sort of tender chide, "why did ye desert me for that other one? In what is she better than I? I should have made 'ee a finer wife, and a more loving one too. 'Tisn't girls that are so easily won at first that are the best. Think how long we've known each other—ever since we were children almost—now haven't we, Tony?"

' "Yes, that we have," says Tony, a-struck with the truth o't.

' "And you've never seen anything in me to complain of, have ye, Tony? Now tell the truth to me?"

' "I never have, upon my life," says Tony.

' "And—can you say I'm not pretty, Tony? Now look at me!"

'He let his eyes light upon her for a long while. "I really can't," says he. ' "In fact, I never knowed you was so pretty before!"

' "Prettier than she?"

'What Tony would have said to that nobody knows, for before he could speak, what should he see ahead, over the hedge past the turning, but a feather he knew well—the feather in Milly's hat— she to whom he had been thinking of putting the question as to giving out the banns that very week.

' "Unity," says he, as mild as he could, "here's Milly coming. Now I shall catch it mightily if she sees 'ee riding here with me; and if you get down she'll be turning the corner in a moment, and, seeing 'ee in the road, she'll know we've been coming on together. Now, dearest Unity, will ye, to avoid all unpleasantness, which I know ye can't bear any more than I, will ye lie down in the back part of the waggon, and let me cover you over with the tarpaulin till Milly has passed? It will all be done in a minute. Do!—and I'll think over what we've said; and perhaps I shall put a loving question to you after all, instead of to Milly. 'Tisn't true that it is all settled between her and me."

'Well, Unity Sallet agreed, and lay down at the back end of the waggon, and Tony covered her over, so that the waggon seemed to be empty but for the loose tarpaulin; and then he drove on to meet Milly.

' "My dear Tony!" cries Milly, looking up with a little pout at him as he came near. "How long you've been coming home! Just as if I didn't live at Upper Longpuddle at all! And I've come to meet you as you asked me to do, and to ride back with you, and talk over our future home—since you asked me, and I promised. But I shouldn't have come else, Mr Tony!"

' "Ay, my dear, I did ask 'ee—to be sure I did, now I think of it—but I had quite forgot it. To ride back with me, did you say, dear Milly?"

' "Well, of course! What can I do else? Surely you don't want me to walk, now I've come all this way?"

' "O no, no! I was thinking you might be going on to town to meet your mother. I saw her there—and she looked as if she might be expecting 'ee.''

' "O no; she's just home. She came across the fields, and so got back before you.''

' "Ah! I didn't know that,'' says Tony. And there was no help for it but to take her up beside him.

'They talked on very pleasantly, and looked at the trees, and beasts, and birds, and insects, and at the ploughmen at work in the fields, till presently who should they see looking out of the upper window of a house that stood beside the road they were following, but Hannah Jolliver, another young beauty of the place at that time, and the very first woman that Tony had fallen in love with— before Milly and before Unity, in fact—the one that he had almost arranged to marry instead of Milly. She was a much more dashing girl than Milly Richards, though he'd not thought much of her of late. The house Hannah was looking from was her aunt's.

' "My dear Milly—my coming wife, as I may call 'ee,'' says Tony in his modest way, and not so loud that Unity could overhear, "I see a young woman a-looking out of window, who I think may accost me. The fact is, Milly, she had a notion that I was wishing to marry her, and since she's discovered I've promised another, and a prettier than she, I'm rather afeard of her temper if she sees us together. Now, Milly, would you do me a favour—my coming wife, as I may say?''

' "Certainly, dearest Tony,'' says she.

' "Then would ye creep under the empty sacks just here in the front of the waggon, and hide there out of sight till we've passed the house? She hasn't seen us yet. You see, we ought to live in peace and good-will since 'tis almost Christmas, and 'twill prevent angry passions rising, which we always should do.''

' "I don't mind, to oblige you, Tony,'' Milly said; and though she didn't care much about doing it, she crept under, and crouched down just behind the seat, Unity being snug at the other end. So they drove on till they got near the road-side cottage. Hannah had soon seen him coming, and waited at the window, looking down upon him. She tossed her head a little disdainful and smiled off-hand.

' "Well, aren't you going to be civil enough to ask me to ride home with you?'' she says, seeing that he was for driving past with a nod and a smile.

'"Ah, to be sure! What was I thinking of?" said Tony, in a flutter. "But you seem as if you was staying at your aunt's?"

'"No, I am not," she said. "Don't you see I have my bonnet and jacket on? I have only called to see her on my way home. How can you be so stupid, Tony?"

'"In that case—ah—of course you must come along wi' me," says Tony, feeling a dim sort of sweat rising up inside his clothes. And he reined in the horse, and waited till she'd come downstairs, and then helped her up beside him. He drove on again, his face as long as a face that was a round one by nature well could be.

'Hannah looked round sideways into his eyes. "This is nice, isn't it, Tony?" she says. "I like riding with you."

'Tony looked back into her eyes. "And I with you," he said after a while. In short, having considered her, he warmed up, and the more he looked at her the more he liked her, till he couldn't for the life of him think why he had ever said a word about marriage to Milly or Unity while Hannah Jolliver was in question. So they sat a little closer and closer, their feet upon the footboard and their shoulders touching, and Tony thought over and over again how handsome Hannah was. He spoke tenderer and tenderer, and called her "dear Hannah" in a whisper at last.

'"You've settled it with Milly by this time, I suppose," said she.

'"N—no, not exactly."

'"What? How low you talk, Tony."

'"Yes—I've a kind of hoarseness. I said, not exactly."

'"I suppose you mean to?"

'"Well, as to that—" His eyes rested on her face, and hers on his. He wondered how he could have been such a fool as not to follow up Hannah. "My sweet Hannah!" he bursts out, taking her hand, not being really able to help it, and forgetting Milly and Unity, and all the world besides. "Settled it? I don't think I have!"

'"Hark!" says Hannah.

'"What?" says Tony, letting go her hand.

'"Surely I heard a sort of little screaming squeak under those sacks? Why, you've been carrying corn, and there's mice in this waggon, I declare!" She began to haul up the tails of her gown.

'"Oh no; 'tis the axle," said Tony in an assuring way. "It do go like that sometimes in dry weather."

'"Perhaps it was.... Well, now, to be quite honest, dear Tony, do you like her better than me? Because—because, although I've held off so independent, I'll own at last that I do like 'ee, Tony, to tell the truth; and I wouldn't say no if you asked me—you know what."

'Tony was so won over by this pretty offering mood of a girl who had been quite the reverse (Hannah had a backward way with her at times, if you can mind) that he just glanced behind, and then whispered very soft, "I haven't quite promised her, and I think I can get out of it, and ask you that question you speak of."

' "Throw over Milly?—all to marry me! How delightful!" broke out Hannah, quite loud, clapping her hands.

'At this there was a real squeak—an angry, spiteful squeak, and afterward a long moan, as if something had broke its heart, and a movement of the empty sacks.

' "Something's there!" said Hannah, starting up.

' "It's nothing, really," says Tony in a soothing voice, and praying inwardly for a way out of this. "I wouldn't tell 'ee at first, because I wouldn't frighten 'ee. But, Hannah, I've really a couple of ferrets in a bag under there, for rabbiting, and they quarrel sometimes. I don't wish it knowed, as 'twould be called poaching. Oh, they can't get out, bless 'ee—you are quite safe! And—and—what a fine day it is, isn't it, Hannah, for this time of year? Be you going to market next Saturday? How is your aunt now?" and so on, says Tony, to keep her from talking any more about love in Milly's hearing.

'But he found his work cut out for him, and wondering again how he should get out of this ticklish business, he looked about for a chance. Nearing home he saw his father in a field not far off, holding up his hand as if he wished to speak to Tony.

' "Would you mind taking the reins a moment, Hannah," he said, much relieved, "while I go and find out what father wants?"

'She consented, and away he hastened into the field, only too glad to get breathing time. He found that his father was looking at him with rather a stern eye.

' "Come, come, Tony," says old Mr Kytes, as soon as his son was alongside him, "this won't do, you know."

' "What?" says Tony.

' "Why, if you mean to marry Milly Richards, do it, and there's an end o't. But don't go driving about the country with

Jolliver's daughter and making a scandal. I won't have such things done."

' "I only asked her—that is, she asked me, to ride home."

' "She? Why, now, if it had been Milly, 'twould have been quite proper; but you and Hannah Jolliver going about by yourselves—"

' "Milly's there too, father."

' "Milly? Where?"

' "Under the corn-sacks! Yes, the truth is, father, I've got rather into a nunny-watch, I'm afeard! Unity Sallet is there too—yes, at the other end, under the tarpaulin. All three are in that waggon, and what to do with 'em I know no more than the dead! The best plan is, as I'm thinking, to speak out loud and plain to one of 'em before the rest, and that will settle it; not but what 'twill cause 'em to kick up a bit of a miff, for certain. Now which would you marry, father, if you was in my place?"

' "Whichever of 'em did *not* ask to ride with thee."

' "That was Milly, I'm bound to say, as she only mounted by my invitation. But Milly—"

' "Then stick to Milly, she's the best ... But look at that!"

'His father pointed toward the waggon. "She can't hold that horse in. You shouldn't have left the reins in her hands. Run on and take the horse's head, or there'll be some accident to them maids!"

'Tony's horse, in fact, in spite of Hannah's tugging at the reins, had started on his way at a brisk walking pace, being very anxious to get back to the stable, for he had had a long day out. Without another word Tony rushed away from his father to overtake the horse.

'Now of all things that could have happened to wean him from Milly there was nothing so powerful as his father's recommending her. No; it could not be Milly, after all. Hannah must be the one, since he could not marry all three as he longed to do. This he thought while running after the waggon. But queer things were happening inside it.

'It was, of course, Milly who had screamed under the sack-bags, being obliged to let off her bitter rage and shame in that way at what Tony was saying, and never daring to show, for very pride and dread o' being laughed at, that she was in hiding. She became more and more restless, and in twisting herself about, what did she see but another woman's foot and white stocking close to her head. It quite frightened her, not knowing that Unity Sallet was in the waggon likewise. But after the fright was over she determined to get to the bottom of all this, and she crept and crept along the bed of the waggon, under the tarpaulin, like a snake, when lo and behold she came face to face with Unity.

' "Well, if this isn't disgraceful!" says Milly in a raging whisper to Unity.

' "'Tis," says Unity, "to see you hiding in a young man's waggon like this, and no great character belonging to either of ye!"

' "Mind what you are saying!" replied Milly, getting louder. "I am engaged to be married to him, and haven't I a right to be here? What right have you, I should like to know? What has he been promising you? A pretty lot of nonsense, I expect! But what Tony says to other women is all mere wind, and no concern to me!"

' "Don't you be too sure!" says Unity. "He's going to have Hannah, and not you, nor me either; I could hear that."

'Now at these strange voices sounding from under the cloth Hannah was thunderstruck a'most into a swound; and it was just at this time that the horse moved on. Hannah tugged away wildly, not knowing what she was doing; and as the quarrel rose louder and louder Hannah got so horrified that she let go the reins altogether. The horse went on at his own pace, and coming to the corner where we turn round to drop down the hill to Lower Longpuddle he turned too quick, the off wheels went up the bank, the waggon rose sideways till it was quite on edge upon the near axles, and out rolled the three maidens into the road in a heap. The horse looked round and stood still.

'When Tony came up, frightened and breathless, he was relieved enough to see that none of his darlings was hurt, beyond a few scratches from the brambles of the hedge. But he was rather alarmed when he heard how they were going on at one another.

' "Don't ye quarrel, my dears—don't ye!" says he, taking off his hat out of respect to 'em. And then he would have kissed them all round, as fair and square as a man could, but they were in too much of a taking to let him, and screeched and sobbed till they was quite spent.

' "Now I'll speak out honest, because I ought to," says Tony, as soon as he could get heard. "And this is the truth," says he. "I've asked Hannah to be mine, and she is willing, and we are going to put up the banns next—"

'Tony had not noticed that Hannah's father was coming up behind, nor had he noticed that Hannah's face was beginning to bleed from the scratch of a bramble. Hannah had seen her father, and had run to him, crying worse than ever.

'"My daughter is *not* willing, sir!" says Mr Jolliver hot and strong. "Be you willing, Hannah? I ask ye to have spirit enough to refuse him, if yer virtue is left to 'ee and you run no risk?"

'"She's as sound as a bell for me, that I'll swear!" says Tony, flaring up. "And so's the others, come to that, though you may think it an onusual thing in me!"

'"I have spirit, and I do refuse him!" says Hannah, partly because her father was there, and partly, too, in a tantrum because of the discovery, and the scratch that might be left on her face. "Little did I think when I was so soft with him just now that I was talking to such a false deceiver!"

'"What, you won't have me, Hannah?" says Tony, his jaw hanging down like a dead man's.

'"Never—I would sooner marry no—nobody at all!" she gasped out, though with her heart in her throat, for she would not have refused Tony if he had asked her quietly, and her father had not been there, and her face had not been scratched by the bramble. And having said that, away she walked upon her father's arm, thinking and hoping he would ask her again.

'Tony didn't know what to say next. Milly was sobbing her heart out; but as his father had strongly recommended her he couldn't feel inclined that way. So he turned to Unity.

'"Well, will you, Unity dear, be mine?" he says.

'"Take her leavings? Not I!" says Unity. "I'd scorn it!" And away walks Unity Sallet likewise, though she looked back when she'd gone some way, to see if he was following her.

'So there at last were left Milly and Tony by themselves, she crying in watery streams, and Tony looking like a tree struck by lightning.

'"Well, Milly," he says at last, going up to her, "it do seem as if fate had ordained that it should be you and I, or nobody. And what must be must be, I suppose. Hey, Milly?"

'"If you like, Tony. You didn't really mean what you said to them?"

'"Not a word of it!" declares Tony, bringing down his fist upon his palm.

'And then he kissed her, and put the waggon to rights, and they mounted together; and their banns were put up the very next Sunday. I was not able to go to their wedding, but it was a rare party they had, by all account.'

Jeff Peters as a Personal Magnet

Jeff Peters has been engaged in as many schemes for making money as there are recipes for cooking in Charleston, S.C.

Best of all I like to hear him tell of his earlier days when he sold liniments and cough cures on street corners, living hand to mouth, heart to heart, with the people, throwing heads or tails with fortune for his last coin.

'I struck Fisher Hill, Arkansaw,' said he, 'in a buckskin suit, moccasins, long hair and a thirty-carat diamond ring that I got from an actor in Texarkana. I don't know what he ever did with the pocket-knife I swapped him for it.

'I was Dr Waugh-hoo, the celebrated Indian medicine man. I carried only one best bet just then, and that was Resurrection Bitters. It was made of life-giving plants and herbs accidentally discovered by Ta-qua-la, the beautiful wife of the chief of the Choctaw Nation, while gathering truck to garnish a platter of boiled dog for the annual corn dance.

'Business hadn't been good at the last town, so I only had five dollars. I went to the Fisher Hill druggist and he credited me for half a gross of eight-ounce bottles and corks. I had the labels and ingredients in my valise, left over from the last town. Life began to look rosy again after I got in my hotel room with the water running from the tap, and the Resurrection Bitters lining up on the table by the dozen.

'Fake? No sir. There was two dollars' worth of fluid extract of cinchoma and a dime's worth of aniline in that half-gross of bitters. I've gone through towns years afterwards and had folks ask for 'em again.

'I hired a wagon that night and commenced selling the bitters on Main Street. Fisher Hill was a low, malarial town; and a compound hypothetical pneumocardiac anti-scorbutic tonic was just what I diagnosed the crowd as needing. The bitters started off like sweetbreads-on-toast at a vegetarian dinner. I had sold two dozen at fifty cents apiece when I felt somebody pull my coat tail. I knew what that meant; so I climbed down and sneaked a five-dollar bill into the hand of a man with a German silver star on his lapel.

' "Constable," says I, "it's a fine night."

' "Have you got a city licence," he asks, "to sell this illegitimate essence of spooju that you flatter by the name of medicine?"

' "I have not," says I. "I didn't know you had a city. If I can find it tomorrow I'll take one out if it's necessary."

' "I'll have to close you up till you do," says the constable.

'I quit selling and went back to the hotel. I was talking to the landlord about it.

' "Oh, you won't stand no show in Fisher Hill," says he. "Dr Hoskins, the only doctor here, is a brother-in-law of the Mayor, and they don't allow no fake doctor to practise in town."

' "I don't practise medicine," says I, "I've got a State pedlar's licence, and I take out a city one wherever they demand it."

'I went to the Mayor's office the next morning and they told me he hadn't showed up yet. They didn't know when he'd be down. So Doc Waugh-hoo hunches down again in a hotel chair and lights a jimpson-weed regalia, and waits.

'By and by a young man in a blue neck-tie slips into the chair next to me and asks the time.

' "Half-past ten," says I, "and you are Andy Tucker. I've seen you work. Wasn't it you that put up the Great Cupid Combination package on the Southern States? Let's see, it was a Chilian diamond engagement ring, a wedding-ring, a potato masher, a bottle of soothing syrup and Dorothy Vernon—all for fifty cents."

'Andy was pleased to hear that I remembered him. He was a good street man; and he was more than that—he respected his profession, and he was satisfied with 300 per cent profit. He had plenty of offers to go into the illegitimate drug and garden seed business; but he was never to be tempted off of the straight path.

'I wanted a partner; so Andy and me agreed to go out together. I told him about the situation in Fisher Hill and how finances was low on account of the local mixture of politics and jalap. Andy had just got in on the train that morning. He was pretty low himself, and was going to canvass the town for a few dollars to build a new battleship by popular subscription at Eureka Springs. So we went out and sat on the porch, and talked it over.

'The next morning at eleven o'clock, when I was sitting there alone, an Uncle Tom shuffles into the hotel and asked for the doctor to come and see Judge Banks, who, it seems, was the mayor and a mighty sick man.

' "I'm no doctor," says I. "Why don't you go and get the doctor?"

' "Boss," says he, "Doc Hoskins am done gone twenty miles in de country to see some sick persons. He's de only doctor in de town, and Massa Banks am powerful bad off. He sent me to ax you to please, suh, come."

' "As man to man," says I, "I'll go and look him over." So I put a bottle of Resurrection Bitters in my pocket and goes up on the hill to the Mayor's mansion, the finest house in town, with a mansard roof and two cast-iron dogs on the lawn.

'This Mayor Banks was in bed all but his whiskers and feet. He was making internal noises that would have had everybody in San Francisco hiking for the parks. A young man was standing by the bed holding a cup of water.

' "Doc," says the Mayor, "I'm awful sick. I'm about to die. Can't you do nothing for me?"

' "Mr Mayor," says I, "I'm not a regular pre-ordained disciple of S. Q. Lapius. I never took a course in a medical college," says I, "I've just come as a fellow-man to see if I could be of assistance."

' "I'm deeply obliged," says he. "Doc Waugh-hoo, this is my nephew, Mr Biddle. He has tried to alleviate my distress, but without success. Oh, Lordy! Ow-ow-ow!!" he sings out.

'I nods at Mr Biddle and sets down by the bed and feels the Mayor's pulse. "Let me see your liver—your tongue, I mean," says I. Then I turns up the lids of his eyes and looks close at the pupils of 'em.

' "How long have you been sick?" I asked.

' "I was taken down—ow-ouch—last night," says the Mayor. "Gimme something for it, doc, won't you?"

' "Mr Fiddle," says I, "raise the window shade a bit, will you?"

' "Biddle," says the young man. "Do you feel like you could eat some ham and eggs, Uncle James?"

' "Mr Mayor," says I, after laying my ear to his right shoulder-blade and listening, "you've got a bad attack of super-inflammation of the right clavicle of the harpsichord!"

' "Good Lord!" says he, with a groan. "Can't you rub something on it, or set it or anything?"

'I picks up my hat and starts for the door.

' "You ain't going, doc?" says the Mayor with a howl. "You

ain't going away and leave me to die with this—superfluity of the clapboards, are you?"

' "Common humanity, Dr Whoa-ha," says Mr Biddle, "ought to prevent your deserting a fellow-human in distress."

' "Dr Waugh-hoo, when you get through ploughing," says I. And then I walks back to the bed and throws back my long hair.

' "Mr Mayor," says I, "there is only one hope for you. Drugs will do you no good. But there is another power higher yet, although drugs are high enough," says I.

' "And what is that?" says he.

' "Scientific demonstrations," says I. "The triumph of mind over sarsaparilla. The belief that there is no pain and sickness except what is produced when we ain't feeling well. Declare yourself in arrears. Demonstrate."

' "What is this paraphernalia you speak of, doc?" says the Mayor. "You ain't a Socialist, are you?"

' "I am speaking," says I, "of the great doctrine of psychic financiering—of the enlightened school of long-distance, subconscientious treatment of fallacies and meningitis—of that wonderful indoor sport known as personal magnetism."

' "Can you work it, doc?" asks the Mayor.

' "I'm one of the Sole Sanhedrims and Ostensible Hooplas of the Inner Pulpit," says I. "The lame talk and the blind rubber whenever I make a pass at 'em. I am a medium, a coloratura hypnotist and a spirituous control. It was only through me at the recent séances at Ann Arbour that the late president of the Vinegar Bitters Company could revisit the earth to communicate with his sister Jane. You see me peddling medicine on the streets," says I, "to the poor. I don't practise personal magnetism on them. I do not drag it in the dust," says I, "because they haven't got the dust."

' "Will you treat my case?" asks the Mayor.

' "Listen," says I. "I've had a good deal of trouble with medical societies everywhere I've been. I don't practise medicine. But, to save your life, I'll give you the psychic treatment if you'll agree as mayor not to push the licence question."

' "Of course I will," says he. "And now get to work, doc, for them pains are coming on again."

' "My fee will be $250, cure guaranteed in two treatments," says I.

' "All right," says the Mayor. "I'll pay it. I guess my life's worth that much."

'I sat down by the bed and looked him straight in the eye.

' "Now," says I, "get your mind off the disease. You ain't sick. You haven't got a heart or a clavicle or a funny-bone or brains or anything. You haven't got any pain. Declare error. Now you feel the pain that you didn't have leaving, don't you?"

' "I do feel some little better, doc," says the Mayor, "darned if I don't. Now state a few lies about my not having this swelling in my left side, and I think I could be propped up and have some sausage and buckwheat cakes."

'I made a few passes with my hands.

' "Now," says I, "the inflammation's gone. The right lobe of the perihelion has subsided. You're getting sleepy. You can't hold your eyes open any longer. For the present the disease is checked. Now, you are asleep."

'The Mayor shut his eyes slowly and began to snore.

' "You observe, Mr Tiddle," says I, "the wonders of modern science."

' "Biddle," says he. "When will you give uncle the rest of the treatment, Dr Pooh-pooh?"

' "Waugh-hoo," says I. "I'll come back at eleven tomorrow. When he wakes up give him eight drops of turpentine and three pounds of steak. Good morning."

'The next morning I went back on time. "Well, Mr Riddle," says I, when he opened the bedroom door, "and how is uncle this morning?"

' "He seems much better," says the young man.

'The Mayor's colour and pulse was fine. I gave him another treatment, and he said the last of the pain left him.

' "Now," says I, "you'd better stay in bed for a day or two, and you'll be all right. It's a good thing I happened to be in Fisher Hill, Mr Mayor," says I, "for all the remedies in the cornucopia that the regular schools of medicine use couldn't have saved you. And now that error has flew and pain proved a perjurer, let's allude to a cheerfuller subject—say the fee of $250. No cheques, please; I hate to write my name on the back of a cheque almost as bad as I do on the front."

' "I've got the cash here," says the Mayor, pulling a pocket-book from under his pillow.

'He counts out five fifty-dollar notes and holds 'em in his hand.

' "Bring the receipt," he says to Biddle.

'I signed the receipt and the Mayor handed me the money. I put it in my inside pocket careful.

' "Now do your duty, officer," says the Mayor, grinning much unlike a sick man.

'Mr Biddle lays his hand on my arm.

' "You're under arrest, Dr Waugh-hoo, alias Peters," says he, "for practising medicine without authority under the State law."

' "Who are you?" I asks.

' "I'll tell you who he is," says Mr Mayor, sitting up in bed. "He's a detective employed by the State Medical Society. He's been following you over five counties. He came to me yesterday and we fixed up this scheme to catch you. I guess you won't do any more doctoring around these parts, Mr Faker. What was it you said I had, doc?" the Mayor laughs, "compound—well it wasn't softening of the brain, I guess, anyway."

' "A detective," says I.

' "Correct," says Biddle. "I'll have to turn you over to the sheriff."

' "Let's see you do it," says I, and I grabs Biddle by the throat and half throws him out of the window, but he pulls a gun and sticks it under my chin, and I stand still. Then he puts handcuffs on me, and takes the money out of my pocket.

' "I witness," says he, "that they're the same bills that you and I marked, Judge Banks. I'll turn them over to the sheriff when we get to his office, and he'll send you a receipt. They'll have to be used as evidence in the case."

' "All right, Mr Biddle," says the Mayor. "And now, Doc Waugh-hoo," he goes on, "why don't you demonstrate? Can't you pull the cork out of your magnetism with your teeth and hocus-pocus them handcuffs off?"

' "Come on, officer," says I, dignified. "I may as well make the best of it." And then I turns to old Banks and rattles my chains.

' "Mr Mayor," says I, "the time will come soon when you'll believe that personal magnetism is a success. And you'll be sure that it succeeded in this case, too."

'And I guess it did.

'When we got nearly to the gate, I says: "We might meet somebody now, Andy. I reckon you better take 'em off, and—" Hey? Why, of course it was Andy Tucker. That was his scheme; and that's how we got the capital to go into business together.'

The Persecution of Bob Pretty

The old man sat on his accustomed bench outside the 'Cauliflower'. A generous measure of beer stood in a blue and white jug by his elbow, and little wisps of smoke curled slowly upwards from the bowl of his churchwarden pipe. The knapsacks of two young men lay where they were flung on the table, and the owners, taking a noontide rest, turned a polite, if bored, ear to the reminiscences of grateful old age.

Poaching, said the old man, who had tried topics ranging from early turnips to horse-racing—poaching ain't wot it used to be, poaching nor anything else; but that there man you might ha' noticed as went out about ten minutes ago and called me 'Old Truthfulness' as 'e passed is the worst one I know. Bob Pretty 'is name is, and of all the sly, artful, deceiving men that ever lived in Claybury 'e is the worst—never did a honest day's work in 'is life, and never wanted the price of a glass of ale.

Bob Pretty's worst time was just after old Squire Brown died. The old squire couldn't afford to preserve much, but by-and-by a gentleman with plenty of money, from London, named Rockett, took 'is place and things began to look up. Pheasants was 'is favourites, and 'e spent no end o' money rearing of 'em, but anything that could be shot at suited 'im, too.

He started by sneering at the little game that Squire Brown 'ad left, but all 'e could do didn't seem to make much difference; things disappeared in a most eggstrordinary way, and the keepers went pretty near crazy, while the things the squire said about Claybury and Claybury men was disgraceful.

Everybody knew as it was Bob Pretty and one or two of 'is mates from other places, but they couldn't prove it. They couldn't catch 'im nohow, and at last the squire 'ad two keepers set off to watch 'im by night and by day.

Bob Pretty wouldn't believe it; he said 'e couldn't. And even when it was pointed out to 'im that Keeper Lewis was follering of 'im he said that it just 'appened he was going the same way, that was all. And sometimes he'd get up in the middle of the night and go for a fifteen-mile walk 'cos 'e'd got the toothache, and Mr Lewis, who 'adn't got it, had to tag along after 'im till he was fit to drop. O' course, it was one keeper the less to look arter the game, and by-the-by the squire see that and took 'im off.

All the same they kept a pretty close watch on Bob, and at last one arternoon they sprang out on 'im as he was walking past Gray's farm, and asked him wot it was he 'ad got in his pockets.

'That's my bisness, Mr Lewis,' ses Bob Pretty.

Mr Smith, the other keeper, passed 'is hands over Bob's coat and felt something soft and bulgy.

'You take your 'ands off of me,' ses Bob; 'you don't know 'ow partikler I am.'

He jerked 'imself away, but they caught 'old of 'im agin, and Mr Lewis put 'is hand in his inside pocket and pulled out two brace o' partridges.

'You'll come along of us,' he ses, catching 'im by the arm.

'We've been looking for you a long time,' ses Keeper Smith, 'and it's a pleasure for us to 'ave your company.'

Bob Pretty said 'e wouldn't go, but they forced 'im along and took 'im all the way to Cudford, four miles off, so that Policeman White could lock 'im up for the night. Mr White was a'most as pleased as the keepers and 'e warned Bob solemn not to speak becos all 'e said would be used agin 'im.

'Never mind about that,' ses Bob Pretty. 'I've got a clear conscience, and talking can't 'urt me. I'm very glad to see you, Mr White; if these two clever, experienced keepers hadn't brought me I should 'ave looked you up myself. They've been and stole my partridges.'

Them as was standing round laughed, and even Policeman White couldn't 'elp giving a little smile.

'There's nothing to laugh at,' ses Bob, 'olding his 'ead up. 'It's a fine thing when a working man—a 'ardworking man—can't take home a little game for 'is family without being stopped and robbed.'

'I s'pose they flew into your pocket?' ses Policeman White.

'No, they didn't,' ses Bob. 'I'm not going to tell lies about it; I put 'em there. The partridges in my inside coat-pocket and the bill in my waistcoat-pocket.'

'The bill?' ses Keeper Lewis, staring at 'im.

'Yes, the bill,' ses Bob Pretty, staring back; 'the bill from Mr Keen, the poulterer, at Wickham.'

He fetched it out of 'is pocket and showed it to Mr White, and the keepers was like madmen a'most 'cos it was plain to see that Bob Pretty 'ad been and bought them partridges just for to play a game on 'em.

'I was curious to know wot they tasted like,' he ses to the policeman. 'Worst of it is, I don't s'pose my pore wife'll know 'ow to cook 'em.'

'You get off 'ome,' ses Policeman White, staring at 'im.

'But ain't I goin' to be locked up?' ses Bob. ' 'Ave I been brought all this way just to 'ave a little chat with a policeman I don't like?'

'You go 'ome,' ses Policeman White, handing the partridges back to 'im.

'All right,' ses Bob, 'and I may 'ave to call you to witness that these 'ere two men laid hold o' me and tried to steal my partridges. I shall go up and see my loryer about it.'

He walked off 'ome with his 'ead up as high as 'e could hold it, and the airs 'e used to give 'imself arter this was terrible for to behold. He got 'is eldest boy to write a long letter to the squire about it, saying that 'e'd overlook it this time, but 'e couldn't promise for the future. Wot with Bob Pretty on one side and Squire Rockett on the other, them two keepers' lives was 'ardly worth living.

Then the squire got a head-keeper named Cutts, a man as was said to know more about the ways of poachers than they did themselves. He was said to 'ave cleared out all the poachers for miles round the place 'e came from, and pheasants could walk into people's cottages and not be touched.

He was a sharp-looking man, tall and thin, with screwed-up eyes and a little red beard. The second day 'e came 'e was up here at this 'ere 'Cauliflower', having a pint o' beer and looking round at the chaps as he talked to the landlord. The odd thing was that men who'd never taken a hare or a pheasant in their lives could 'ardly meet 'is eye, while Bob Pretty stared at 'im as if 'e was a wax-works.

'I 'ear you 'ad a little poaching in these parts afore I came,' ses Mr Cutts to the landlord.

'I think I 'ave 'eard something o' the kind,' ses the landlord, staring over his 'ead with a far-away look in 'is eyes.

'You won't hear of much more,' ses the keeper. 'I've invented a new way of catching the dirty rascals; afore I came 'ere I caught all the poachers on three estates. I clear 'em out just like a ferret clears out rats.'

'Sort o' man-trap?' ses the landlord.

'Ah, that's tellings,' ses Mr Cutts.

'Well, I 'ope you'll catch 'em here,' ses Bob Pretty; 'ther's far too many of 'em about for my liking. Far too many.'

'I shall 'ave 'em afore long,' ses Mr Cutts, nodding his 'ead.

'Your good 'ealth,' ses Bob Pretty, holding up 'is mug. 'We've been wanting a man like you for a long time.'

'I don't want any of your impidence, my man,' ses the keeper. 'I've 'eard about you, and nothing good either. You be careful.'

'I am careful,' ses Bob, winking at the others. 'I 'ope you'll catch all them low poaching chaps; they give the place a bad name, and I'm a'most afraid to go out arter dark for fear o' meeting 'em.'

Peter Gubbins and Sam Jones began to laugh, but Bob Pretty got angry with 'em and said he didn't see there was anything to laugh at. He said that poaching was a disgrace to their native place, and instead o' laughing they ought to be thankful to Mr Cutts for coming to do away with it all.

'Any help I can give you shall be given cheerful,' he ses to the keeper.

'When I want your help I'll ask you for it,' ses Mr Cutts.

'Thankee,' ses Bob Pretty. 'I on'y 'ope I sha'n't get my face knocked about like yours 'as been, that's all; cos my wife's so partikler.'

'Wot d'ye mean?' ses Mr Cutts, turning on him. 'My face ain't been knocked about.'

'Oh, I beg your pardin,' ses Bob; 'I didn't know it was natural.'

Mr Cutts went black in the face a'most and stared at Bob Pretty as if 'e was going to eat 'im, and Bob stared back, looking fust at the keeper's nose and then at 'is eyes and mouth, and then at 'is nose agin.

'You'll know me agin, I s'pose?' ses Mr Cutts, at last.

'Yes,' ses Bob, smiling; 'I should know you a mile off—on the darkest night.'

'We shall see,' ses Mr Cutts, taking up 'is beer and turning 'is back on him. 'Those of us as live the longest'll see the most.'

'I'm glad I've lived long enough to see 'im,' ses Bob to Bill Chambers. 'I feel more satisfied with myself now.'

Bill Chambers coughed, and Mr Cutts, arter finishing 'is beer, took another look at Bob Pretty, and went off boiling a'most.

The trouble he took to catch Bob Pretty arter that you wouldn't believe, and all the time the game seemed to be simply melting away, and Squire Rockett was finding fault with 'im all day long. He was worn to a shadder a'most with watching, and Bob Pretty seemed to be more prosperous than ever.

Sometimes Mr Cutts watched in the plantations, and sometimes 'e hid 'imself near Bob's house, and at last one night, when 'e was crouching behind the fence of Frederick Scott's front garden, 'e saw Bob Pretty come out of 'is house and, arter a careful look round, walk up the road. He held 'is breath as Bob passed 'im, and was just getting up to foller 'im when Bob stopped and walked slowly back agin, sniffing.

'Wot a delicious smell o' roses!' he ses out loud.

He stood in the middle o' the road nearly opposite where the keeper was hiding, and sniffed so that you could ha' heard him the other end o' the village.

'It can't be roses,' he ses, in a puzzled voice, 'becos there ain't no roses hereabouts, and besides, it's too late for 'em. It must be Mr Cutts, the clever new keeper.'

He put his 'ead over the fence and bid 'im good evening, and said wot a fine night for a stroll it was, and asked 'im whether 'e was waiting for Frederick Scott's aunt. Mr Cutts didn't answer 'im a word; 'e was pretty near bursting with passion. He got up and shook 'is fist in Bob Pretty's face, and then 'e went off stamping down the road as if 'e was going mad.

And for a time Bob Pretty seemed to 'ave all the luck on 'is side. Keeper Lewis got rheumatic fever, which 'e put down to sitting about night arter night in damp places watching for Bob, and, while 'e was in the thick of it, with the doctor going every day, Mr Cutts fell in getting over a fence and broke 'is leg. Then all the work fell on Keeper Smith, and to 'ear 'im talk you'd think that rheumatic fever and broken legs was better than anything else in the world. He asked the squire for 'elp, but the squire wouldn't give it to 'im, and he kept telling 'im wot a feather in 'is cap it would be if 'e did wot the other two couldn't do, and caught Bob Pretty. It was all very well, but, as Smith said, wot 'e wanted was feathers in 'is piller, instead of 'aving to snatch a bit o' sleep in 'is chair or sitting down with his 'ead agin a tree. When I tell you that 'e fell asleep in this public-'ouse one night while the landlord was drawing a pint o' beer he 'ad ordered, you'll know wot 'e suffered.

O' course, all this suited Bob Pretty as well as could be, and he was that good-tempered 'e'd got a nice word for everybody, and when Bill Chambers told 'im 'e was foolhardy 'e only laughed and said 'e knew wot 'e was about.

But the very next night 'e had reason to remember Bill Chambers's words. He was walking along Farmer Hall's field—the one next to the squire's plantation—and, so far from being nervous, 'e was actually a-whistling. He'd got a sack over 'is shoulder, loaded as full as it could be, and 'e 'ad just stopped to light 'is pipe when three men burst out o' the plantation and ran towards 'im as 'ard as they could run.

Bob Pretty just gave one look and then 'e dropped 'is pipe and set off like a hare. It was no good dropping the sack, because Smith, the keeper, 'ad recognized 'im and called 'im by name, so 'e just put 'is teeth together and did the best he could, and there's no doubt that if it 'adn't ha' been for the sack 'e could 'ave got clear away.

As it was, 'e ran for pretty near a mile, and they could 'ear 'im breathing like a pair o' bellows; but at last 'e saw that the game was up. He just managed to struggle as far as Farmer Pinnock's pond, and then, waving the sack round his 'ead, 'e flung it into the middle of it, and fell down gasping for breath.

'Got—you—this time—Bob Pretty,' ses one o' the men, as they came up.

'Wot—*Mr Cutts*?' ses Bob, with a start.

'That's me, my man,' ses the keeper.

'Why—I thought—you was— Is that *Mr Lewis*? It can't be.'

'That's me,' ses Keeper Lewis. 'We both got well suddenlike, Bob Pretty, when we 'eard you was out. You ain't so sharp as you thought you was.'

Bob Pretty sat still, getting 'is breath back and doing a bit o' thinking at the same time.

'You give me a start,' he ses, at last. 'I thought you was both in bed, and, knowing 'ow hard worked Mr Smith 'as been, I just came round to 'elp 'im keep watch like. I promised to 'elp you, Mr Cutts, if you remember.'

'Wot was that you threw in the pond just now?' ses Mr Cutts.

'A sack,' ses Bob Pretty; 'a sack I found in Farmer Hall's field. It felt to me as though it might 'ave birds in it, so I picked it up, and I was just on my way to your 'ouse with it, Mr Cutts, when you started arter me.'

'Ah!' ses the keeper, 'and wot did you run for?'

Bob Pretty tried to laugh. 'Becos I thought it was the poachers arter me,' he ses. 'It seems ridiklous, don't it?'

'Yes, it does,' ses Lewis.

'I thought you'd know me a mile off,' ses Mr Cutts. 'I should ha' thought the smell o' roses would ha' told you I was near.'

Bob Pretty scratched 'is 'ead and looked at 'im out of the corner of 'is eye, but he 'adn't got any answer. Then 'e sat biting his finger-nails and thinking, while the keepers stood argyfying as to who should take 'is clothes off and go into the pond arter the pheasants. It was a very cold night and the pond was pretty deep in places, and none of 'em seemed anxious.

'Make 'im go in for it,' ses Lewis, looking at Bob; ' 'e chucked it in.'

'On'y becos I thought you was poachers,' ses Bob. 'I'm sorry to have caused so much trouble.'

'Well, you go in and get it out,' ses Lewis, who pretty well guessed who'd 'ave to do it if Bob didn't. 'It'll look better for you, too.'

'I've got my defence all right,' ses Bob Pretty. 'I ain't set a foot on the squire's preserves, and I found this sack a 'undered yards away from it.'

'Don't waste more time,' ses Mr Cutts to Lewis. 'Off with your clothes and in with you. Anybody'd think you was afraid of a little cold water.'

'Whereabouts did 'e pitch it in?' ses Lewis.

Bob Pretty pointed with 'is finger exactly where 'e thought it was, but they wouldn't listen to 'im, and then Lewis, arter twice saying wot a bad cold he'd got, took 'is coat off very slow and careful.

'I wouldn't mind going in to oblige you,' ses Bob Pretty, 'but the pond is so full o' them cold, slimy efts; I don't fancy them crawling up agin me, and, besides that, there's such a lot o' deep holes in it. And wotever you do don't put your 'ead under; you know 'ow foul that water is.'

Keeper Lewis pretended not to listen to 'im. He took off 'is clothes very slowly and then 'e put one foot in and stood shivering, although Smith, who felt the water with his 'and, said it was quite warm. Then Lewis put the other foot in and began to walk about careful, arf-way up to 'is knees.

'I can't find it,' he ses, with 'is teeth chattering.

'You 'aven't looked,' ses Mr Cutts; 'walk about more; you can't expect to find it all at once. Try the middle.'

Lewis tried the middle, and 'e stood there up to 'is neck, feeling more with his foot and saying things out loud about Bob Pretty, and other things under 'is breath about Mr Cutts.

'Well, I'm going off 'ome,' ses Bob Pretty, getting up. 'I'm too tender-'earted to stop and see a man drownded.'

'You stay 'ere,' ses Mr Cutts, catching 'old of him.

'Wot for?' ses Bob; 'you've got no right to keep me 'ere.'

'Catch 'old of 'im, Joe,' ses Mr Cutts, quick-like.

Smith caught 'old of his other arm, and Lewis left off trying to find the sack to watch the struggle. Bob Pretty fought 'ard, and once or twice 'e nearly tumbled Mr Cutts into the pond, but at last he gave in and lay down panting and talking about 'is loryer. Smith 'eld him down on the ground while Mr Cutts kept pointing out places with 'is finger for Lewis to walk to. The last place 'e pointed to wanted a much taller man, but it wasn't found out till too late, and the fuss Keeper Lewis made when 'e could speak agin was terrible.

'You'd better come out,' ses Mr Cutts; 'you ain't doing no good. We know where they are and we'll watch the pond till daylight— that is, unless Smith 'ud like to 'ave a try.'

'It's pretty near daylight now, I think,' ses Smith.

Lewis came out and ran up and down to dry 'imself, and finished off on his pocket-'andkerchief, and then with 'is teeth chattering 'e began to dress 'imself. He got 'is shirt on, and then 'e stood turning over 'is clothes as if 'e was looking for something.

'Never mind about your stud now,' ses Mr Cutts; 'hurry up and dress.'

'Stud?' ses Lewis, very snappish. 'I'm looking for my trowsis.'

'Your trowsis?' ses Smith, 'elping 'im look.

'I put all my clothes together,' ses Lewis, a'most shouting. 'Where are they? I'm 'arf perished with cold. Where are they?'

'He 'ad 'em on this evening,' ses Bob Pretty, ''cos I remember noticing 'em.'

'They must be somewhere about,' ses Mr Cutts; 'why don't you use your eyes?'

He walked up and down, peering about, and as for Lewis he was 'opping round 'arf crazy.

'I wonder,' ses Bob Pretty, in a thoughtful voice, to Smith—'I wonder whether you or Mr Cutts kicked 'em in the pond while you was struggling with me. Come to think of it, I seem to remember 'earing a splash.'

'He's done it, Mr Cutts,' ses Smith; 'never mind, it'll go all the 'arder with 'im.'

'But I do mind,' ses Lewis shouting, 'I'll be even with you for this, Bob Pretty. I'll make you feel it. You wait till I've done with you. You'll get a month extra for this, you see if you don't.'

'Don't you mind about me,' ses Bob; 'you run off 'ome and cover them legs of yours. I found that sack, so my conscience is clear.'

Lewis put on 'is coat and waistcoat and set off, and Mr Cutts and Smith, arter feeling about for a dry place, set theirselves down and began to smoke.

'Look 'ere,' ses Bob Pretty, 'I'm not going to sit 'ere all night to please you; I'm going off 'ome. If you want me you'll know where to find me.'

'You stay where you are,' ses Mr Cutts. 'We ain't going to let you out of our sight.'

'Very well, then, you take me 'ome,' ses Bob. 'I'm not going to catch my death o' cold sitting 'ere. I'm not used to being out of a night like you are. I was brought up respectable.'

'I daresay,' ses Mr Cutts. 'Take you 'ome, and then 'ave one o' your mates come and get the sack while we're away.'

Then Bob Pretty lost 'is temper, and the things 'e said about Mr Cutts wasn't fit for Smith to hear. He threw 'imself down at last full length on the ground and sulked till the day broke.

Keeper Lewis was there a'most as soon as it was light, with some long hay-rakes he borrowed, and I should think that pretty near 'arf the folks in Claybury 'ad turned up to see the fun. Mrs Pretty was crying and wringing 'er 'ands; but most folk seemed to be rather pleased that Bob 'ad been caught at last.

In next to no time 'arf-a-dozen rakes was at work and the things they brought out o' that pond you wouldn't believe. The edge of it was all littered with rusty tin pails and sauce-pans and such-like, and by-and-by Lewis found the things he'd 'ad to go 'ome without a few hours afore, but they didn't seem to find that sack, and Bob Pretty, wot was talking to 'is wife, began to look 'opeful.

But just then the squire came riding up with two friends as was staying with 'im, and he offered a reward of five shillings to the man wot found it. Three or four of 'em waded in up to their middle then and raked their 'ardest, and at last Henery Walker give a cheer and brought it to the side, all heavy with water.

'That's the sack I found, sir,' ses Bob, starting up. 'It wasn't on your land at all, but on the field next to it. I'm an honest, 'ardworking man, and I've never been in trouble afore. Ask anybody 'ere and they'll tell you the same.'

Squire Rockett took no notice of 'im. 'Is that the sack?' he asks, turning to Mr Cutts.

'That's the one, sir,' ses Mr Cutts. 'I'd swear to it anywhere.'

'You'd swear a man's life away,' ses Bob. ''Ow can you swear to it when it was dark?'

Mr Cutts didn't answer 'im. He went down on 'is knees and cut the string that tied up the mouth o' the sack, and then 'e started back as if 'e'd been shot, and 'is eyes a'most started out of 'is 'ead.

'What's the matter?' ses the squire.

Mr Cutts couldn't speak; he could only stutter and point at the sack with 'is finger, and Henery Walker, as was getting curious, lifted up the other end of it and out rolled about a score of as fine cabbages as you could wish to see.

I never see people so astonished afore in all my born days, and as for Bob Pretty 'e stood staring at them cabbages as if 'e couldn't believe 'is eyesight.

'And that's wot I've been kept 'ere all night for,' he ses at last, shaking his 'ead. 'That's wot comes o' trying to do a kindness to keepers, and 'elping of 'em in their difficult work. P'r'aps that ain't the sack arter all, Mr Cutts. I could ha' sworn they was pheasants in the one *I* found, but I may be mistook, never 'aving 'ad one in my 'ands afore. Or p'r'aps somebody was trying to 'ave a game with you, Mr Cutts, and deceived me instead.'

The keepers on'y stared at 'im.

'You ought to be more careful,' ses Bob. 'Very likely while you was taking all that trouble over me, and Keeper Lewis was catching 'is death o' cold, the poachers was up at the plantation taking all they wanted. And, besides, it ain't right for Squire Rockett to 'ave to pay Henery Walker five shillings for finding a lot of old cabbages. I shouldn't like it myself.'

He looked out of the corner of 'is eye at the squire, as was pretending not to notice Henery Walker touching 'is cap to him, and then 'e turns to 'is wife and he ses,

'Come along, old gal,' 'e ses. 'I want my breakfast bad, and arter that I shall 'ave to lose a honest day's work in bed.'

UB

A few weeks ago there was an item of news about a man in America who was arrested for continually running into shiny new cars with his jalopy (this excellent word, pronounced to rhyme with, but not associated with 'sloppy', is the American expression for an old car). When asked for an explanation he replied simply 'I just don't like 'em.'

How I agree with that man! I should like to take him out in UB. UB is the name of my car, which is not only a jalopy but has these fascinating letters in its registration. UB is pronounced to rhyme and is sometimes associated with 'pub'. It is inconceivable that my car should be called AD, or BO, or MO, let alone anything Polish or Czechoslovakian like KX or ZB. It is as much UB as a mangle is a mangle.

I bought it before the war for £7 from a clerkly sort of man who had bought it brand-new in 1928. He could hardly have gone out much in it, because he had spent every week-end doing the weekly tasks laid down in the instruction book. It was almost the same as on the day it rolled off the assembly line, when this now grey-haired man was a conveyancer, or perhaps an assayer.

On second thoughts I am pretty sure it didn't come off an assembly line at all. Cars like UB were made lovingly, one at a time, by elderly, shirt-sleeved craftsmen such as one used to see in the drawings of Mr Heath Robinson—men who only twenty years previously had been building gigs, traps and phaetons. One can tell this from the position of the headlights, which are at the side of the windscreen. People who do not understand about UB ask me sarcastically where I get the acetylene these days, but that is only because they are peeved at not being able to find the battery, which is under the passenger's seat. I always see UB taking shape in a place which I visualize as a converted barn still filled with a faint smell of musty hay. Dust floats in the sunbeams filtering through a small, high window. The craftsmen are in consultation. 'Gideon,' says one of them, 'let us have an oil-gauge in this one.'

His mate looks perturbed. 'You know what we said about not buying anything outside, Eli,' he says.

'Nay, Gideon, it is a thing we can make ourselves. I thought of it as I was coming through Barton's Copse this morning. Lookee here.' And he goes on to explain UB's oil-gauge.

It is for this alone that I would rather have UB than my friend Harblow's car, in which the dashboard is a mass of instruments. For my oil-gauge is not an instrument at all. It is a button. You start the engine and press this button in. If it comes out again you know the oil pressure is all right. Either it is all right or it isn't. There is none of this worrying about falling below a certain pressure (and I suspect that most people, like Harblow, don't know what this pressure is supposed to be, anyway).

It is the same with the rest of the car. Harblow would never, in his most boastful moments, say he really understands his carburettor, which has about five pipes going into it and also has an absurd frying-pan thing full of *oil* on the top, which he says lamely is an *air-cleaner*. UB has been bumbling along now for twenty years with the good old British atmosphere, which is clean enough for us. And whoever heard of cleaning air, or anything else for that matter, with *oil*? Gideon, Eli and Co. knew better. They knew that a carburettor is essentially a thing with holes in it for mixing petrol and air in a fine spray ready for explosion, and they didn't go messing about with things full of oil, which would obviously find its way eventually to these holes and block them up, in much the same way as marmalade always finds its way between one's fingers. And there is one pipe going into my carburettor. You know where you are.

Harblow's car has the petrol tank at the back. It is connected to the engine, which is much higher up and about ten feet away, by a complicated system of pipes and taps and pumps and filters (there seems to be a mania for filtering and cleaning in modern cars). Any one of these things can go wrong, and usually does, about twelve miles from Swindon on a dark wet night. Whenever I am with him it is a thing called the automatic pump. We can't even begin to repair it until the engine has cooled down because it is right in the bowels of the mechanism and one burns one's knuckles against the hot cylinder block. This pump seems to have about a hundred washers, which either get dropped and lost or are discovered to have been left out when the whole thing has been tightened up again. After half an hour's sucking, blowing and cursing Harblow produces a little wire gauze thing full of the most amazing geological specimens. 'The filter is choked,' he says indignantly. 'This petrol is a scandal.' Well, I buy the same petrol and it doesn't choke my filter because there isn't one. I have a theory that a strange chemical action takes place in these filters and that the petrol crystallizes out. Gideon and Eli didn't have to worry about pumps, automatic or otherwise, because UB's petrol tank is behind the dashboard and the stuff just *falls* down according to the well-known laws of Isaac Newton.

Then there are the brakes. Every three months or so Harblow notices a funny smell and he gets out and finds that his rear brake linings are practically on fire. He has hydraulic brakes (*more* pipes and, I shouldn't be surprised, more filters) and to put them right it is necessary to perform a terrible operation called bleeding the master cylinder. UB's brakes, although a considerable advance in their day on the earlier models of Gideon and Eli, which probably had a stout oak block against the wheel rim operated by iron levers. are simplicity itself. They are operated by wire cables which pass over a little wheel coming down on a screw thing from the floor of the car. If the brakes are too tight you screw the wheel down a bit. It takes one minute. Bleeding the master cylinder takes Harblow three week-ends at home and then two months in a garage.

Another thing of which people like Harblow seem to be inordinately proud is the fact that their engines are mounted on rubber. It is true that when he starts up his car during his eternal attentions to the innumerable cleaners, boosters, dust-baths, bird-bins and fly-traps the whole engine does jump about in a most insecure-looking fashion, so that you can see about ten of it. But it seems very precious to me. UB's engine is bolted firmly to the chassis, and when it is ticking over it is the mudguards of which you see about ten; there is a nice comfortable thubbing feeling as you get into the seat. Rubber is perishable, and this is one of the many reasons why you often see cars like Harblow's on scrap heaps but never cars like UB. It is because the owners have got tired of bleeding the master cylinder and adjusting the oil-filter, the petrol-filter and the air-filter and buying new blocks of rubber. You couldn't have left one of these rubber-mounted cars at the bottom of the garden throughout the whole war, as I did UB, and found it ready to drive again after fitting a new hood, new plugs, new windscreen-wiper (and, come to think of it, a new windscreen), two new tyres, new king-pins, new front spring, new cylinder head, new battery, re-wiring and re-painting, drying out the magneto in the oven, getting the dynamo re-wound and mending the leaks in the radiator.

You would have found the rubber had perished.

Soaked in Seaweed or Upset in the Ocean (An old-fashioned sea story)

It was in August in 1867 that I stepped on board the deck of the *Saucy Sally*, lying in dock at Gravesend, to fill the berth of second mate.

Let me first say a word about myself.

I was a tall, handsome young fellow, squarely and powerfully built, bronzed by the sun and the moon (and even copper-coloured in spots from the effect of the stars), and with a face in which honestly, intelligence, and exceptional brain power were combined with Christianity, simplicity, and modesty.

As I stepped on the deck I could not help a slight feeling of triumph, as I caught sight of my sailor-like features reflected in a tar-barrel that stood beside the mast, while a little later I could scarcely repress a sense of gratification as I noticed them reflected again in a bucket of bilge water.

'Welcome on board, Mr Blowhard,' called out Captain Bilge, stepping out of the binnacle and shaking hands across the taffrail.

I saw before me a fine sailor-like man of from thirty to sixty, clean-shaven, except for an enormous pair of whiskers, a heavy beard, and a thick moustache, powerful in build, and carrying his beam well aft, in a pair of broad duck trousers across the back of which there would have been room to write a history of the British Navy.

Beside him were the first and third mates, both of them being quiet men of poor stature, who looked at Captain Bilge with what seemed to me an apprehensive expression in their eyes.

The vessel was on the eve of departure. Her deck presented that scene of bustle and alacrity dear to the sailor's heart. Men were busy nailing up the masts, hanging the bowsprit over the side, varnishing the lee-scuppers and pouring hot tar down the companion-way.

Captain Bilge, with a megaphone to his lips, kept calling out to the men in his rough sailor fashion:

'Now, then, don't over-exert yourselves, gentlemen. Remember, please, that we have plenty of time. Keep out of the sun as much as you can. Step carefully in the rigging there, Jones; I fear it's just a little high for you. Tut, tut, Williams, don't get yourself so dirty with that tar, you won't look fit to be seen.'

I stood leaning over the gaff of the mainsail and thinking—yes, thinking, dear reader, of my mother. I hope that you will think none the less of me for that. Whenever things look dark, I lean up against something and think of mother. If they get positively black, I stand on one leg and think of father. After that I can face anything.

Did I think, too, of another, younger than mother and fairer than father? Yes, I did. 'Bear up, darling,' I had whispered as she nestled her head beneath my oilskins and kicked out backward with one heel in the agony of her girlish grief, 'in five years the voyage will be over, and after three more like it, I shall come back with money enough to buy a second-hand fishing-net and settle down on shore.'

Meantime the ship's preparations were complete. The masts were all in position, the sails nailed up, and men with axes were busily chopping away the gangway.

'All ready?' called the Captain.

'Aye, aye, sir.'

'Then hoist the anchor in board and send a man down with the key to open the bar.'

Opening the bar! the last sad rite of departure. How often in my voyages have I seen it; the little group of men soon to be exiled from their home, standing about with saddened faces, waiting to see the man with the key open the bar—held there by some strange fascination.

Next morning with a fair wind astern we had buzzed around the corner of England and were running down the Channel.

I know no finer sight, for those who have never seen it, than the English Channel. It is the highway of the world. Ships of all nations are passing up and down, Dutch, Scotch, Venezuelan, and even American.

Chinese junks rush to and fro. Warships, motor yachts, icebergs, and lumber rafts are everywhere. If I add to this fact that so thick a fog hangs over it that it is entirely hidden from sight, my readers can form some idea of the majesty of the scene.

We had now been three days at sea. My first sea-sickness was wearing off, and I thought less of father.

On the third morning Captain Bilge descended to my cabin.
'Mr Blowhard,' he said, 'I must ask you to stand double watches.'

'What is the matter?' I inquired.

'The two other mates have fallen overboard,' he said uneasily, and avoiding my eye.

I contented myself with saying, 'Very good, sir,' but I could not help thinking it a trifle odd that both the mates should have fallen overboard in the same night.

Surely there was some mystery in this.

Two mornings later the Captain appeared at the breakfast-table with the same shifting and uneasy look in his eye.

'Anything wrong, sir?' I asked.

'Yes,' he answered, trying to appear at ease and twisting a fried egg to and fro between his fingers with such nervous force as almost to break it in two—'I regret to say that we have lost the bosun.'

'The bosun!' I cried.

'Yes,' said Captain Bilge more quietly, 'he is overboard. I blame myself for it, partly. It was early this morning. I was holding him up in my arms to look at an iceberg, and, quite accidentally I assure you—I dropped him overboard.'

'Captain Bilge,' I asked, 'have you taken any steps to recover him?'

'Not as yet,' he replied uneasily.

I looked at him fixedly, but said nothing.

Ten days passed.

The mystery thickened. On Thursday two men of the starboard watch were reported missing. On Friday the carpenter's assistant disappeared. On the night of Saturday a circumstance occurred which, slight as it was, gave me some clue as to what was happening.

As I stood at the wheel about midnight, I saw the Captain approach in the darkness carrying the cabin-boy by the hind leg. The lad was a bright little fellow, whose merry disposition had already endeared him to me, and I watched with some interest to see what the Captain would do to him. Arrived at the stern of the vessel, Captain Bilge looked cautiously around a moment and then dropped the boy into the sea. For a brief instant the lad's head appeared in the phosphorus of the waves. The Captain threw a boot at him, sighed deeply, and went below.

Here then was the key to the mystery! The Captain was throwing the crew overboard. Next morning we met at breakfast as usual.

'Poor little Williams has fallen overboard,' said the Captain, seizing a strip of ship's bacon and tearing at it with his teeth as if he almost meant to eat it.

'Captain,' I said, greatly excited, stabbing at a ship's loaf in my agitation with such ferocity as almost to drive my knife into it— 'You threw that boy overboard!'

'I did,' said Captain Bilge, grown suddenly quiet, 'I threw them all over and intend to throw the rest. Listen, Blowhard, you are young, ambitious, and trustworthy. I will confide in you.'

Perfectly calm now, he stepped to a locker, rummaged in it a moment, and drew out a faded piece of yellow parchment, which he spread on the table. It was a map or chart. In the centre of it was a circle. In the middle of the circle was a small dot and a letter T, while at one side of the map was a letter N, and against it on the other side a letter S.

'What is this?' I asked.

'Can you not guess?' queried Captain Bilge. 'It is a desert island.'

'Ah!' I rejoined with a sudden flash of intuition, 'and N is for North and S is for South.'

'Blowhard,' said the Captain, striking the table with such force as to cause a loaf of ship's bread to bounce up and down three or four times, 'you've struck it. That part of it had not yet occurred to me.'

'And the letter T?' I asked.

'The treasure, the buried treasure,' said the Captain, and turning the map over he read from the back of it—'The point T indicates the spot where the treasure is buried under the sand; it consists of half a million Spanish dollars, and is buried in a brown leather dress-suit case.'

'And where is the island?' I inquired, mad with excitement.

'That I do not know,' said the Captain. 'I intend to sail up and down the parallels of latitude until I find it.'

'And meantime?'

'Meantime, the first thing to do is to reduce the number of the crew so as to have fewer hands to divide among. Come, come,' he added in a burst of frankness which made me love the man in spite of his short comings, 'will you join me in this? We'll throw them all over, keeping the cook to the last, dig up the treasure, and be rich for the rest of our lives.'

Reader, do you blame me if I said yes? I was young, ardent, ambitious, full of bright hopes and boyish enthusiasm.

'Captain Bilge,' I said, putting my hand in his, 'I am yours.'

'Good,' he said, 'now go forward to the forecastle and get an idea what the men are thinking.'

I went forward to the men's quarters—a plain room in the front of the ship, with only a rough carpet on the floor, a few simple armchairs, writing-desks, spittoons of a plain pattern, and small brass beds with blue-and-green screens. It was Sunday morning, and the men were mostly sitting about in their dressing gowns.

They rose as I entered and curtseyed.

'Sir,' said Tompkins, the bosun's mate, 'I think it is my duty to tell you that there is a great deal of dissatisfaction among the men.'

Several of the men nodded.

'They don't like the way the men keep going overboard,' he continued, his voice rising to a tone of uncontrolled passion. 'It is positively absurd, sir, and if you will allow me to say so, the men are far from pleased.'

'Tompkins,' I said sternly, 'you must understand that my position will not allow me to listen to mutinous language of this sort.'

I returned to the Captain. 'I think the men mean mutiny,' I said.

'Good,' said Captain Bilge, rubbing his hands, 'that will get rid of a lot of them, and of course,' he added musingly, looking out of the broad old-fashioned port-hole at the stern of the cabin at the heaving waves of the South Atlantic, 'I am expecting pirates at any time, and that will take out quite a few of them. However'—and here he pressed the bell for a cabin-boy—'kindly ask Mr Tompkins to step this way.'

'Tompkins,' said the Captain as the bosun's mate entered, 'be good enough to stand on the locker and stick your head through the stern port-hole, and tell me what you think of the weather.'

'Aye, aye, sir,' replied the tar with a simplicity which caused us to exchange a quiet smile.

Tompkins stood on the locker and put his head and shoulders out of the port.

Taking a leg each we pushed him through. We heard him plump into the sea.

'Tompkins was easy,' said Captain Bilge. 'Excuse me as I enter his death in the log.'

'Yes,' he continued presently, 'it will be a great help if they mutiny. I suppose they will, sooner or later. It's customary to do so. But I shall take no step to precipitate it until we have first fallen in with pirates. I am expecting them in these latitudes at any time. Meantime, Mr Blowhard,' he said, rising, 'if you can continue to drop overboard one or two more each week, I shall feel extremely grateful.'

Three days later we rounded the Cape of Good Hope and entered upon the inky waters of the Indian Ocean. Our course lay now in zigzags and, the weather being favourable, we sailed up and down at a furious rate over a sea as calm as glass.

On the fourth day a pirate ship appeared. Reader, I do not know if you have ever seen a pirate ship. The sight was one to appal the stoutest heart. The entire ship was painted black, a black flag hung at the masthead, the sails were black, and on the deck people dressed all in black walked up and down arm-in-arm. The words 'Pirate Ship' were painted in white letters on the bow. At the sight of it our crew were visibly cowed. It was a spectacle that would have cowed a dog.

The two ships were brought side by side. They were then lashed tightly together with bag string and binder twine, and a gang plank laid between them. In a moment the pirates swarmed upon our deck, rolling their eyes, gnashing their teeth and filing their nails.

Then the fight began. It lasted two hours—with fifteen minutes off for lunch. It was awful. The men grappled with one another, kicked one another from behind, slapped one another across the face, and in many cases completely lost their temper and tried to bite one another. I noticed one gigantic fellow brandishing a knotted towel, and striking right and left among our men, until Captain Bilge rushed at him and struck him flat across the mouth with a banana skin.

At the end of two hours, by mutual consent, the fight was declared a draw. The points standing at sixty-one and a half against sixty-two.

The ships were unlashed, and with three cheers from each crew, were headed on their way.

'Now, then,' said the Captain to me aside, 'let us see how many of the crew are sufficiently exhausted to be thrown overboard.'

He went below. In a few minutes he returned, his face deadly pale. 'Blowhard,' he said, 'the ship is sinking. One of the pirates (sheer accident, of course, I blame no one) has kicked a hole in the side. Let us sound the well.'

We put our ear to the ship's well. It sounded like water.

The men were put to the pumps and worked with the frenzied effort which only those who have been drowned in a sinking ship can understand.

At six p.m. the well marked one half an inch of water, at nightfall three-quarters of an inch, and at daybreak, after a night of unremitting toil, seven-eighths of an inch.

By noon of the next day the water had risen to fifteen-sixteenths of an inch, and on the next night the sounding showed thirty-one thirty-seconds of an inch of water in the hold. The situation was desperate. At this rate of increase few, if any, could tell where it would rise to in a few days.

That night the Captain called me to his cabin. He had a book of mathematical tables in front of him, and great sheets of vulgar fractions littered the floor on all sides.

'The ship is bound to sink,' he said, 'in fact, Blowhard, she is sinking. I can prove it. It may be six months or it may take years, but if she goes on like this, sink she must. There is nothing for it but to abandon her.'

That night, in the dead of darkness, while the crew were busy at the pumps, the Captain and I built a raft.

Unobserved we cut down the masts, chopped them into suitable lengths, laid them crosswise in a pile and lashed them tightly together with bootlaces.

Hastily we threw on board a couple of boxes of food and bottles of drinking fluid, a sextant, a chronometer, a gas-meter, a bicycle pump and a few other scientific instruments. Then taking advantage of a roll in the motion of the ship, we launched the raft, lowered ourselves upon a line and under cover of the heavy dark of a tropical night, we paddled away from the doomed vessel.

The break of day found us a tiny speck on the Indian Ocean. We looked about as big as this (.).

In the morning, after dressing, and shaving as best we could, we opened our box of food and drink.

Then came the awful horror of our situation.

One by one the Captain took from the box the square blue tins of canned beef which it contained. We counted fifty-two in all. Anxiously and with drawn faces we watched until the last can was lifted from the box. A single thought was in our minds. When the end came the Captain stood up on the raft with wild eyes staring at the sky.

'The can-opener!' he shrieked, 'just Heaven, the can-opener.' He fell prostrate.

Meantime, with trembling hands, I opened the box of bottles. It contained lager beer bottles, each with a patent tin top. One by one I took them out. There were fifty-two in all. As I withdrew the last one and saw the empty box before me, I shroke out—'The thing! the thing! oh, merciful Heaven! The thing you open them with!'

I fell prostrate upon the Captain.

We awoke to find ourselves still a mere speck upon the ocean. We felt even smaller than before.

Over us was the burnished copper sky of the tropics. The heavy, leaden sea lapped the sides of the raft. All about us was a litter of corn beef cans and lager beer bottles. Our sufferings in the ensuing days were indescribable. We beat and thumped at the cans with our fists. Even at the risk of spoiling the tins for ever we hammered them fiercely against the raft. We stamped on them, bit at them and swore at them. We pulled and clawed at the bottles with our hands, and chipped and knocked them against the cans, regardless even of breaking the glass and ruining the bottles.

It was futile.

Then day after day we sat in moody silence, gnawed with hunger, with nothing to read, nothing to smoke, and practically nothing to talk about.

On the tenth day the Captain broke silence.

'Get ready the lots, Blowhard,' he said. 'It's got to come to that.'

'Yes,' I answered drearily, 'we're getting thinner every day.'

Then, with the awful prospect of cannibalism before us, we drew lots.

I prepared the lots and held them to the Captain. He drew the longer one.

'Which does that mean,' he asked, trembling between hope and despair. 'Do I win?'

'No, Bilge,' I said sadly, 'you lose.'

But I mustn't dwell on the days that followed—the long quiet days of lazy dreaming on the raft, during which I slowly built up my strength, which had been shattered by privation. They were days, dear reader, of deep and quiet peace, and yet I cannot recall them without shedding a tear for the brave man who made them what they were.

It was on the fifth day after that I was awakened from a sound sleep by the bumping of the raft against the shore. I had eaten perhaps overheartily, and had not observed the vicinity of land.

Before me was an island, the circular shape of which, with its low, sandy shore, recalled at once its identity.

'The treasure island,' I cried, 'at last I am rewarded for all my heroism.'

In a fever of haste I rushed to the centre of the island. What was the sight that confronted me? A great hollow scooped in the sand, an empty dress-suit case lying beside it, and on a ship's plank driven deep in the sand, the legend, '*Saucy Sally*, October, 1867.' So! the miscreants had made good the vessel, headed it for the island of whose existence they must have learned from the chart we so carelessly left on the cabin table, and had plundered poor Bilge and me of our well-earned treasure!

Sick with the sense of human ingratitude I sank upon the sand.

The island became my home.

There I eked out a miserable existence, feeding on sand and gravel and dressing myself in cactus plants. Years passed. Eating sand and mud slowly undermined my robust constitution. I fell ill. I died. I buried myself.

Would that others who write sea stories would do as much.

Frank O'Connor

First Confession

All the trouble began when my grandfather died and my grand-mother—my father's mother—came to live with us. Relations in the one house are a strain at the best of times, but, to make matters worse, my grandmother was a real old country-woman and quite unsuited to the life in town. She had a fat, wrinkled old face, and, to Mother's great indignation, went round the house in bare feet—the boots had her crippled, she said. For dinner she had a jug of porter and a pot of potatoes with—sometimes—a bit of salt fish, and she poured out the potatoes on the table and ate them slowly, with great relish, using her fingers by way of a fork.

Now, girls are supposed to be fastidious, but I was the one who suffered most from this. Nora, my sister, just sucked up to the old woman for the penny she got every Friday out of the old-age pension, a thing I could not do. I was too honest, that was my trouble; and when I was playing with Bill Connell, the sergeant-major's son, and saw my grandmother steering up the path with the jug of porter sticking out from beneath her shawl, I was mortified. I made excuses not to let him come into the house, because I could never be sure what she would be up to when we went in.

When Mother was at work and my grandmother made the dinner I wouldn't touch it. Nora once tried to make me, but I hid under the table from her and took the bread-knife with me for protection. Nora let on to be very indignant (she wasn't, of course, but she knew Mother saw through her, so she sided with Gran) and came after me. I lashed out at her with the bread-knife, and after that she left me alone. I stayed there till Mother came in from work and made my dinner, but when Father came in later Nora said in a shocked voice: 'Oh, Dadda, do you know what Jackie did at dinner-time?' Then, of course, it all came out; Father gave me a flaking; Mother interfered, and for days after that he didn't speak to me and Mother barely spoke to Nora. And all because of that old woman! God knows I was heart-scalded.

Then, to crown my misfortunes, I had to make my first con-fession and communion. It was an old woman called Ryan who prepared us for these. She was about the one age with Gran; she was well-to-do, lived in a big house on Montenotte, wore a black cloak and bonnet, and came every day to school at three o'clock when we should have been going home, and talked to us of hell. She may have mentioned the other place as well, but that could only have been by accident, for hell had the first place in her heart.

She lit a candle, took out a new half-crown, and offered it to the first boy who would hold one finger—only one finger!—in the flame for five minutes by the school clock. Being always very ambitious I was tempted to volunteer, but I thought it might look greedy. Then she asked were we afraid of holding one—only one finger!—in a little candle flame for five minutes and not afraid of burning all over in roasting hot furnaces for all eternity. 'All eternity! Just think of that! A whole lifetime goes by and it's nothing, not even a drop in the ocean of your sufferings.' The woman was really interesting about hell, but my attention was all fixed on the half-crown. At the end of the lesson she put it back in her purse. It was a great disappointment; a religious woman like that, you wouldn't think she'd bother about a thing like a half-crown.

Another day she said she knew a priest who woke one night to find a fellow he didn't recognize leaning over the end of his bed. The priest was a bit frightened—naturally enough—but he asked the fellow what he wanted, and the fellow said in a deep, husky voice that he wanted to go to confession. The priest said it was an awkward time and wouldn't it do in the morning, but the fellow said that last time he went to confession, there was one sin he kept back, being ashamed to mention it, and now it was always on his mind. Then the priest knew it was a bad case, because the fellow was making a bad confession and committing a mortal sin. He got up to dress, and just then the cock crew in the yard outside, and—lo and behold!—when the priest looked round there was no sign of the fellow, only a smell of burning timber, and when the priest looked at his bed didn't he see the print of two hands burned in it? That was because the fellow had made a bad confession. This story made a shocking impression on me.

But the worst of all was when she showed us how to examine our conscience. Did we take the name of the Lord, our God, in vain? Did we honour our father and our mother? (I asked her did this include grandmothers and she said it did.) Did we love our neighbours as ourselves? Did we covet our neighbour's goods? (I thought of the way I felt about the penny that Nora got every

Friday.) I decided that, between one thing and another, I must have broken the whole ten commandments, all on account of that old woman, and so far as I could see, so long as she remained in the house I had no hope of ever doing anything else.

I was scared to death of confession. The day the whole class went I let on to have a toothache, hoping my absence wouldn't be noticed; but at three o'clock, just as I was feeling safe, along comes a chap with a message from Mrs Ryan that I was to go to confession myself on Saturday and be at the chapel for communion with the rest. To make it worse, Mother couldn't come with me and sent Nora instead.

Now, that girl had ways of tormenting me that Mother never knew of. She held my hand as we went down the hill, smiling sadly and saying how sorry she was for me, as if she were bringing me to the hospital for an operation.

'Oh, God help us!' she moaned. 'Isn't it a terrible pity you weren't a good boy? Oh, Jackie, my heart bleeds for you! How will you ever think of all your sins? Don't forget you have to tell him about the time you kicked Gran on the shin.'

'Lemme go!' I said, trying to drag myself free of her. 'I don't want to go to confession at all.'

'But sure, you'll have to go to confession, Jackie,' she replied in the same regretful tone. 'Sure, if you didn't, the parish priest would be up to your house, looking for you. 'Tisn't, God knows, that I'm not sorry for you. Do you remember the time you tried to kill me with the bread-knife under the table? And the language you used to me? I don't know what he'll do with you at all, Jackie. He might have to send you up to the bishop.'

I remember thinking bitterly that she didn't know the half of what I had to tell—if I told it. I knew I couldn't tell it, and understood perfectly why the fellow in Mrs Ryan's story made a bad confession; it seemed to me a great shame that people wouldn't stop criticizing him. I remember that steep hill down to the church, and the sunlit hillsides beyond the valley of the river, which I saw in the gaps between the houses like Adam's last glimpse of Paradise.

Then, when she had manoeuvred me down the long flight of steps to the chapel yard, Nora suddenly changed her tone. She became the raging malicious devil she really was.

'There you are!' she said with a yelp of triumph, hurling me through the church door. 'And I hope he'll give you the penitential psalms, you dirty little caffler.'

I knew then I was lost, given up to eternal justice. The door with the coloured-glass panels swung shut behind me, the sunlight went out and gave place to deep shadow, and the wind whistled outside so that the silence within seemed to crackle like ice under my feet. Nora sat in front of me by the confession box. There were a couple of old women ahead of her, and then a miserable-looking poor devil came and wedged me in at the other side, so that I couldn't escape even if I had the courage. He joined his hands and rolled his eyes in the direction of the roof, muttering aspirations in an anguished tone, and I wondered had he a grandmother too. Only a grandmother could account for a fellow behaving in that heart-broken way, but he was better off than I, for he at least could go and confess his sins; while I would make a bad confession and then die in the night and be continually coming back and burning people's furniture.

Nora's turn came, and I heard the sound of something slamming, and then her voice as if butter wouldn't melt in her mouth, and then another slam, and out she came. God, the hypocrisy of women! Her eyes were lowered, her head was bowed, and her hands were joined very low down on her stomach, and she walked up the aisle to the side altar looking like a saint. You never saw such an exhibition of devotion; and I remembered the devilish malice with which she had tormented me all the way from our door, and wondered were all religious people like that, really. It was my turn now. With the fear of damnation in my soul I went in, and the confessional door closed of itself behind me.

It was pitch-dark and I couldn't see priest or anything else. Then I really began to be frightened. In the darkness it was a matter between God and me, and He had all the odds. He knew what my intentions were before I even started; I had no chance. All I had ever been told about confession got mixed up in my mind, and I knelt to one wall and said: 'Bless me, father, for I have sinned; this is my first confession.' I waited for a few minutes, but nothing happened, so I tried it on the other wall. Nothing happened there either. He had me spotted all right.

It must have been then that I noticed the shelf at about one height with my head. It was really a place for grown-up people to rest their elbows, but in my distracted state I thought it was probably the place you were supposed to kneel. Of course, it was on the high side and not very deep, but I was always good at climbing and managed to get up all right. Staying up was the trouble.

There was room only for my knees, and nothing you could get a grip on but a sort of wooden moulding a bit above it. I held on to the moulding and repeated the words a little louder, and this time something happened all right. A slide was slammed back; a little light entered the box, and a man's voice said: 'Who's there?'

' 'Tis me, father,' I said for fear he mightn't see me and go away again. I couldn't see him at all. The place the voice came from was under the moulding, about level with my knees, so I took a good grip of the moulding and swung myself down till I saw the astonished face of a young priest looking up at me. He had to put his head on one side to see me, and I had to put mine on one side to see him, so we were more or less talking to one another upside-down. It struck me as a queer way of hearing confessions, but I didn't feel it my place to criticize.

'Bless me, father, for I have sinned; this is my first confession,' I rattled off all in one breath, and swung myself down the least shade more to make it easier for him.

'What are you doing up there?' he shouted in an angry voice, and the strain the politeness was putting on my hold of the moulding, and the shock of being addressed in such an uncivil tone were too much for me. I lost my grip, tumbled, and hit the door an unmerciful wallop before I found myself flat on my back in the middle of the aisle. The people who had been waiting stood up with their mouths open. The priest opened the door of the middle box and came out, pushing his biretta back from his forehead; he looked something terrible. Then Nora came scampering down the aisle.

'Oh, you dirty little caffler!' she said. 'I might have known you'd do it. I might have known you'd disgrace me. I can't leave you out of my sight for one minute.'

Before I could even get to my feet to defend myself she bent down and gave me a clip across the ear. This reminded me that I was so stunned I had even forgotten to cry, so that people might think I wasn't hurt at all, when in fact I was probably maimed for life. I gave a roar out of me.

'What's all this about?' the priest hissed, getting angrier than ever and pushing Nora off me. 'How dare you hit the child like that, you little vixen?'

'But I can't do my penance with him, father,' Nora cried, cocking an outraged eye up at him.

'Well, go and do it, or I'll give you some more to do,' he said, giving me a hand up. 'Was it coming to confession you were, my poor man?' he asked me.

' 'Twas, father,' said I with a sob.

'Oh,' he said respectfully, 'a big hefty fellow like you must have terrible sins. Is this your first?'

' 'Tis, father,' said I.

'Worse and worse,' he said gloomily. 'The crimes of a life-time. I don't know will I get rid of you at all today. You'd better wait now till I'm finished with these old ones. You can see by the looks of them they haven't much to tell.'

'I will, father,' I said with something approaching joy.

The relief of it was really enormous. Nora stuck out her tongue at me from behind his back, but I couldn't even be bothered retorting. I knew from the very moment that man opened his mouth that he was intelligent above the ordinary. When I had to think, I saw how right I was. It only stood to reason that a fellow confessing after seven years would have more to tell than people that went every week. The crimes of a lifetime, exactly as he said. It was only what he expected, and the rest was the cackle of old women and girls with their talk of hell, the bishop, and the penitential psalms. That was all they knew. I started to make my examination of conscience, and barring the one bad business of my grandmother it didn't seem so bad.

The next time, the priest steered me into the confession box himself and left the shutter back the way I could see him get in and sit down at the further side of the grille from me.

'Well, now,' he said, 'what do they call you?'

'Jackie, father,' said I.

'And what's a-trouble to you, Jackie?'

'Father,' I said, feeling I might as well get it over while I had him in good humour, 'I had it all arranged to kill my grandmother.'

He seemed a bit shaken by that, all right, because he said nothing for quite a while.

'My goodness,' he said at last, 'that'd be a shocking thing to do. What put that into your head?'

'Father,' I said, feeling very sorry for myself, 'she's an awful woman.'

'Is she?' he asked. 'What way is she awful?'

'She takes porter, father,' I said, knowing well from the way

Mother talked of it that this was a mortal sin, and hoping it would make the priest take a more favourable view of my case.

'Oh, my!' he said, and I could see he was impressed.

'And snuff, father,' said I.

'That's a bad case, sure enough, Jackie,' he said.

'And she goes round in her bare feet, father,' I went on in a rush of self-pity, 'and she knows I don't like her, and she gives pennies to Nora and none to me, and my da sides with her and flakes me, and one night I was so heart-scalded I made up my mind I'd have to kill her.'

'And what would you do with the body?' he asked with great interest.

'I was thinking I could chop that up and carry it away in a barrow I have,' I said.

'Begor, Jackie,' he said, 'do you know you're a terrible child?'

'I know, father,' I said, for I was just thinking the same thing myself. 'I tried to kill Nora too with a bread-knife under the table, only I missed her.'

'Is that the little girl that was beating you just now?' he asked.

' 'Tis, father,'

'Someone will go for her with a bread-knife one day, and he won't miss her,' he said rather cryptically. 'You must have great courage. Between ourselves, there's a lot of people I'd like to do the same to but I'd never have the nerve. Hanging is an awful death.'

'Is it, father?' I asked with the deepest interest—I was always very keen on hanging. 'Did you ever see a fellow hanged?'

'Dozens of them,' he said solemnly. 'And they all died roaring.'

'Jay!' I said.

'Oh, a horrible death!' he said with great satisfaction. 'Lots of the fellows I saw killed their grandmothers too, but they all said 'twas never worth it.'

He had me there for a full ten minutes talking, and then walked out the chapel yard with me. I was genuinely sorry to part with him, because he was the most entertaining character I'd ever met in the religious line. Outside, after the shadow of the church, the sunlight was like the roaring of waves on a beach; it dazzled me; and when the frozen silence melted and I heard the screech of trams on the road my heart soared. I knew now I wouldn't die in the night and come back, leaving marks on my mother's furniture. It would be a great worry to her, and the poor soul had enough.

Nora was sitting on the railing, waiting for me, and she put on a very sour puss when she saw the priest with me. She was mad jealous because a priest had never come out of the church with her.

'Well,' she asked coldly, after he left me, 'what did he give you?'

'Three Hail Marys,' I said.

'Three Hail Marys,' she repeated incredulously. 'You mustn't have told him anything.'

'I told him everything,' I said confidently.

'About Gran and all?'

'About Gran and all.'

(All she wanted was to be able to go home and say I'd made a bad confession.)

'Did you tell him you went for me with the bread-knife?' she asked with a frown.

'I did to be sure,'

'And he only gave you three Hail Marys?'

'That's all.'

She slowly got down from the railing with a baffled air. Clearly, this was beyond her. As we mounted the steps back to the main road she looked at me suspiciously.

'What are you sucking?' she asked.

'Bullseyes.'

'Was it the priest gave them to you?'

''Twas.'

'Lord God,' she wailed bitterly, 'some people have all the luck! 'Tis no advantage to anybody trying to be good. I might just as well be a sinner like you.'

The Oompa

You know that very tricky bit for the trombone in Liszt's Second Hungarian Rhapsody. It is very uplifting and has given a certain dignity to an instrument that is too often on the squalid side and prone to buffoonery.

But I hate the sound of it. The Second Hungarian Rhapsody was the test piece in the Inter-Counties Brass Band Contest in 1932. The Meadow Prospect Jubilee Band was thought before the contest to be a firm favourite. We had attained a unique swing and cohesion under our conductor, Elmo Lucroft. The leading gambler in Meadow Prospect, Kitchener Bowen, told us that we had practically ousted horses as objects of gambling.

Our strongest card was our first trombonist. In his hand the instrument lost all its oafishness and raced along like a strong, perfectly trained voice. And in that Hungarian Rhapsody he trod on the slopes of glory. Liszt had been waiting for just this boy. Then two months before the contest he accepted a post in the extreme north of England in the research branch of a soap works. We supposed that his fifteen years on the trombone had made him some potent kind of bubble blower. We were bitter and very down on soap, and we strongly criticized Kitchener Bowen who had first drawn the attention of the trombonist to the advertisement printed by the soap works.

Kitchener Bowen and his chief accountant in the bookie business, Offa Cule, were with us one night in the snug of the Picton. Kitchener was telling us that his faith in us still stood sky-high and that he was taking in a lot of betting money on us, and he was determined to find us a brilliant replacement for the man who had gone north in soap.

'What is all this?' asked Offa Cule, looking blank. Offa, while a magician with sums of money that have horses attached to them, touched the cultural life of Meadow Prospect only when driven into it by a high wind.

Kitchener explained our problem.

'Oh, that's easy,' said Offa. 'Is that all you want, a trombone player?' and he chuckled as if he had a queue of them lined up in the back yard of the Picton. 'Here in Meadow Prospect you have the greatest trombonist who ever lived. Uriah Dyer.'

We looked at Teilo Dew, who is a walking *Debrett* of Meadow Prospect bandsmen. If you've ever sat on a platform or in a park and played through an entire piece of band music you are somewhere in Teilo Dew's mental files.

'Offa's raving,' said Teilo. 'If there is a trombone player in this town called Uriah Dyer he must have done all his playing at midnight, in disguise and muted to the last degree.'

'Dyer did his playing in a place called Fernlea to the south of here. And that's his name, Uriah Dyer.'

'Let's see him,' said Kitchener and off we went.

Offa led us to one of the steepest streets in the zone and marched us upward with that fast lope which he had found the best gait for quick movement through a sub-moral life.

Teilo Dew paused half-way up the hill, pulled us to a halt and pointed thoughtfully at Offa. 'Uriah Dyer,' he said. 'There never was anybody with a name like that. This is some kind of pointless jest played by Cule there to discourage bandsmen.'

We stopped in front of the top house. We were high up. The air was rare and sharp. Offa gave the door a bang. It was opened so swiftly the tenant might either have been waiting for us to call or had come rushing through the passage to keep the door from falling in after receiving that powerful clip from Cule.

'This is Uriah Dyer,' said Offa, and we all gave him a courteous bow.

Dyer was a small pensive man with none of the panache that one associates with triumphant players of the more blaring instruments.

'We are desperately short of a good trombone player,' said Kitchener, 'and we have been told you may help us.'

Dyer motioned us into a small front room and we grouped ourselves around him waiting for him to speak his first word.

Dyer stared across the room at the picture of a man wearing a Salvation Army uniform. We followed his eyes but he stayed silent.

'Now,' said Teilo Dew, 'he will ask what's a trombone. Nobody living this high on a hill could bear to stand the touch of metal on the lip.' He shook his head towards Offa Cule. 'Morally that Cule is an acrobat. He's out to bewilder life and he's doing very well.'

'Did you ever play the trombone, Mr Dyer?'

'Oh, yes. A long time ago.'

'Of course he did,' said Offa. 'My uncle in Fernlea says that Uriah Dyer at his best could do things with the slide trombone that would have brought Jack Teagarden to the boil.'

Uriah Dyer brought us some tea.

'Do you play now?'

'I promised my father that I would never lay lip to trombone again. It was a sacred promise.'

We sipped the tea. It was very weak and we could believe the stories we had heard of tea-leaves floating right out of the pot at certain heights above sea level. We all urged Dyer to explain.

'You remember that 1908 was a bad year for Fernlea?'

'Yes,' said Teilo Dew, a natural chronicler. 'There was blood on the moon that year all right. Two floods, one explosion, a landslide that blotted out a street and three Slate Club secretaries collided as they met at the railway station door.'

'That's it. Trouble from every quarter.'

'In which of these calamities were you involved, Mr Dyer?'

'Directly in none of them. We lived high on the hillside there as here. My father was a smallholder and a greengrocer who went around the place selling his produce from a cart. We helped him. So we were not in the pit to be blown up nor in the bottom of the valley to be drowned or buried. We were in the Salvation Army Band. I was the trombonist. My father played the trumpet. He had little ear but he could play loud and was a useful all-weather player. My brother was the drummer. We were a fair band, one of the best ever to play in the single cause of godliness. The disasters hit the band badly. My father, my brother and I were the only survivors. My brother and I assumed that we could never play again.'

We all nodded to show that we would have been with the Dyer brothers on that point.

'But Dad marched us down to the Fernlea Square on Saturday night when the sinners are noisy and rampant and bold. The unbelievers came from every gloomy corner of Fernlea to laugh at us and taunt us. I suppose we looked daft, just the three of us, blowing and banging away, a rag, a remnant, you might say, of what had been a very great sound. It was drizzling, too, and too much humidity around the mouthpiece always made my father slip off the note, and he caused my brother on the drum to sound very muffled and uncertain. It was a field day for the scoffers and agnostics of the town. How, they asked, and they came up close to ask it, how could we have faith in a providence that allowed a whole band to be filleted in this fashion, leaving such a small and gruesome rump? They charged us with being just arrant exhibitionists out to make a show at all costs. My brother and I gave up the ghost. I stopped blowing. He stopped banging. Then my father started. He was half-mad with rage. He began clouting the two of us with his trumpet and said that if we fell into silence in the face of such dark forces he would beat our brains out, and his last act would be a rough rendering of "Lead Kindly Light" on a bent horn.'

Uriah Dyer puckered his lips as if he had been touched by some physical sensation recalled from that period.

'And that happened,' he said, 'every Saturday night for twelve months.'

Teilo Dew, who had kept his slouch on as part of his cautious policy of sad disengagement, now took it off to show respect.

'Time and again my brother and I would give up in defeat, but my father would lash us back into life. It wore him out. If not he would surely have finished us off for he was a dervish when he had that trumpet in his hand and rage in his heart. I got to play very fine. The better I played the less likely I was to be clouted half silly by my father's trumpet. Before he died he said he was sorry and ashamed for the way he treated us. He admitted that since the vanishing of the band's main body his own personal faith had taken a few deep dents, and made us swear that we would never again play the trombone or the drum. My brother burned his drum.'

'And you,' said Teilo in the hollow voice he uses when he seems to be seeing life turn black in the face, 'and you buried your trombone?'

'No, I still have it.'

He went to a cupboard. He brought out a trombone. It looked battered as if Dyer might at times have done a bit of counter-belting when his father came around with the trumpet.

'Your old man would want you to do this for us,' said Kitchener. 'A bandsman's loyalty to bandsmanship overrides any promise, however sacred.'

'All right,' said Dyer, 'I'll do it. I rather fancy having the feel of this thing in my hands again. There's only one proviso.'

'Anything you say.'

'No rehearsals. You've got to take my word for it that during that ordeal with my old man I became one of the greatest trombonists of all time. My lips and my lungs have lost none of their magic. Just send the car for me when you are ready to take the stage for the contest. When you hear me go into that boom-boom-boom solo piece in the Rhapsody, Liszt will smile again. Oh, and one more thing, send me a copy of the music.'

We had to agree.

On the day of the contest Dyer was sent for and he had the air of an emperor as he walked on to the platform. He was swinging his trombone as gaily as a Hawaiian bouquet. Elmo Lucroft was staring at him with an intensity of distrust that only a dedicated band leader ever manages to get lastingly on to his face.

'I don't like it,' he said to me. 'No one has ever heard him play a note. If it weren't for my early Sunday School training I'd have gone through with my original plan of smuggling in a professional.'

We started. Lucroft stationed me near Dyer to check his progress and to give him encouragement if he should need it. There were several notes for the trombone and I leaned over Dyer to get a gauge of his quality. Dyer lifted the instrument and was very confidently distending his cheeks but I did not hear a sound.

'Try shaking it, Dyer,' I said. 'There may be something nesting in the pipes after all those years in that cupboard.'

'No, no,' he whispered. 'I had a run through this morning. Sweet as a nut. Every note a hallelujah. It'll be all right in time for the big solo part.'

But I noticed that he started shaking his instrument all the same for all his talk of sweetness and nuts. He smiled at the other bandsmen around him and they frowned back, thinking Dyer to be a buffoon. I heard a few faint notes when Dyer tried again but they were thin and totally unplanned by Liszt.

We came up to the big trombone solo. Dyer was pale and nervous now and his eyes were taking in a few of the angrier bandsmen who had their instruments raised offensively against him. He muttered to me that being surrounded by all that brass and racket and being stared at by Lucroft had brought back to him all the terrors of those lost Saturday nights.

'Stand up for your big piece,' I told him, 'if you think that that will enable you to let it rip a little more boldly.'

He did that and let fly with one of the loudest notes I have ever heard. It was the most terrifying and disruptive oompa since the first marriage of music and metal. Lucroft ducked behind his stand as if he thought that Dyer was now firing at him, and Teilo Dew, who was in charge of the sleigh bells at the back, hit his apparatus over with a clatter that put the Rhapsody flat on its back. I pulled Dyer back on to his chair and threatened to kill him if he played another note.

Of course we lost and the Birchtown Brass won. We saw Kitchener Bowen rush on to the conductor of the Birchtown Brass and he and Dyer were laughing in the friendliest way as they left the marquee arm in arm and made tracks for the Picton.

Kitchener, they say, bought a new car with his winnings. Lucroft saved up and bought something for himself. He came into rehearsal with a smile of the lowest possible candle and dandling a new baton. This baton, he explained, had a filling of lead shot and he would use it only for the longer dirges and for that golden evening when Dyer would again be drawn by memory of that sombre catharsis in 1908 to turn up once again among us bandsmen.

About Kitchener Bowen I ask only this. How deep can a person get and still want to return to the surface to plague his fellows?

James Thurber

The Secret Life of Walter Mitty

'We're going through!' The Commander's voice was like thin ice breaking. He wore his full-dress uniform, with the heavily braided white cap pulled down rakishly over one cold grey eye. 'We can't make it, sir. It's spoiling for a hurricane, if you ask me.' 'I'm not asking you, Lieutenant Berg,' said the Commander. 'Throw on the power lights! Rev her up to 8,500! We're going through!' The pounding of the cylinders increased: ta-pocketa-pocketa-pocketa *pocketa-pocketa*. The Commander stared at the ice forming on the pilot window. He walked over and twisted a row of complicated dials. 'Switch on No. 8 auxiliary!' he shouted. 'Switch on No. 8 auxiliary!' repeated Lieutenant Berg. 'Full strength in No. 3 turret!' shouted the Commander. 'Full strength in No. 3 turret!' The crew, bending to their various tasks in the huge, hurtling eight-engined Navy hydroplane, looked at each other and grinned. 'The Old Man'll get us through,' they said to one another. 'The Old Man ain't afraid of Hell!'

'Not so fast! You're driving too fast!' said Mrs Mitty. 'What are you driving so fast for?'

'Hmm?' said Walter Mitty. He looked at his wife, in the seat beside him, with shocked astonishment. She seemed grossly unfamiliar, like a strange woman who had yelled at him in a crowd. 'You were up to fifty-five,' she said. 'You know I don't like to go more than forty. You were up to fifty-five.' Walter Mitty drove on toward Waterbury in silence, the roaring of the SN 202 through the worst storm in twenty years of Navy flying fading in the remote, intimate airways of his mind. 'You're tensed up again,' said Mrs Mitty. 'It's one of your days. I wish you'd let Dr Renshaw look you over.'

Walter Mitty stopped the car in front of the building where his wife went to have her hair done. 'Remember to get those overshoes while I'm having my hair done,' she said. 'I don't need overshoes,' said Mitty. She put her mirror back into her bag. 'We've been all through that,' she said, getting out of the car. 'You're not a young man any longer.' He raced the engine a little. 'Why don't you wear your gloves? Have you lost your gloves?' Walter Mitty reached in a pocket and brought out the gloves. He put them on, but after she had turned and gone into the building and he had driven on to a red light, he took them off again. 'Pick it up, brother!' snapped a cop as the light changed, and Mitty hastily pulled on his gloves and lurched ahead. He drove around the streets aimlessly for a time, and then he drove past the hospital on his way to the parking lot.

... 'It's the millionaire banker, Wellington McMillan,' said the pretty nurse. 'Yes?' said Walter Mitty, removing his gloves slowly. 'Who has the case?' 'Dr Renshaw and Dr Benbow, but there are two specialists here, Dr Remington from New York and Mr Pritchard-Mitford from London. He flew over.' A door opened down a long, cool corridor and Dr Renshaw came out. He looked distraught and haggard. 'Hello, Mitty,' he said. 'We're having the devil's own time with McMillan, the millionaire banker and close personal friend of Roosevelt. Obstreosis of the ductal tract. Tertiary. Wish you'd take a look at him.' 'Glad to,' said Mitty.

In the operating room there were whispered introductions: 'Dr Remington, Dr Mitty. Mr Pritchard-Mitford, Dr Mitty.' 'I've read your book on streptothricosis,' said Pritchard-Mitford, shaking hands. 'A brilliant performance, sir.' 'Thank you,' said Walter Mitty. 'Didn't know you were in the States, Mitty,' grumbled Remington. 'Coals to Newcastle, bringing Mitford and me up here for a tertiary.' 'You are very kind,' said Mitty. A huge, complicated machine, connected to the operating table, with many tubes and wires, began at this moment to go pocketa-pocketa-pocketa. 'The new anaesthetizer is giving way!' shouted an interne. 'There is no one in the East who knows how to fix it!' 'Quiet, man!' said Mitty, in a low, cool voice. He sprang to the machine, which was now going pocketa-pocketa-queep-pocketa-queep. He began fingering delicately a row of glistening dials. 'Give me a fountain-pen!' he snapped. Someone handed him a fountain-pen. He pulled a faulty piston out of the machine and inserted the pen in its place. 'That will hold for ten minutes,' he said. 'Get on with the operation.' A nurse hurried over and whispered to Renshaw, and Mitty saw the man turn pale. 'Coreopsis has set in,' said Renshaw nervously. 'If you would take over, Mitty?' Mitty looked at him and at the craven figure of Benbow, who drank, and at the grave, uncertain faces of the two great specialists. 'If you wish,' he said. They slipped a white gown on him; he adjusted a mask and drew on thin gloves; nurses handed him shining...

'Back it up, Mac! Look out for that Buick!' Walter Mitty jammed on the brakes. 'Wrong lane, Mac,' said the parking-lot attendant, looking at Mitty closely. 'Gee. Yeh,' muttered Mitty. He began cautiously to back out of the lane marked 'Exit Only.' 'Leave her sit here,' said the attendant. 'I'll put her away.' Mitty got out of the car. 'Hey, better leave the key.' 'Oh,' said Mitty, handing the man the ignition key. The attendant vaulted into the car, backed it up with insolent skill, and put it where it belonged.

They're so damn cocky, thought Walter Mitty, walking along Main Street; they think they know everything. Once he had tried to take his chains off, outside New Milford, and he had got them wound around the axles. A man had had to come out in a wrecking car and unwind them, a young, grinning garageman. Since then Mrs Mitty always made him drive to a garage to have the chains taken off. The next time, he thought, I'll wear my right arm in a sling; they won't grin at me then. I'll have my right arm in a sling and they'll see I couldn't possibly take the chains off myself. He kicked at the slush on the sidewalk. 'Overshoes,' he said to himself, and he began looking for a shoe store.

When he came out into the street again, with the overshoes in a box under his arm, Walter Mitty began to wonder what the other thing was his wife had told him to get. She had told him twice, before they set out from their house for Waterbury. In a way he hated these weekly trips to town—he was always getting something wrong. Kleenex, he thought, Squibb's, razor blades? No. Toothpaste, toothbrush, bicarbonate, carborundum, initiative and referendum? He gave it up. But she would remember it. 'Where's the what's-its-name?' she would ask. 'Don't tell me you forgot the what's-its-name.' A newsboy went by shouting something about the Waterbury trial.

... 'Perhaps this will refresh your memory.' The District Attorney suddenly thrust a heavy automatic at the quiet figure on the witness stand. 'Have you ever seen this before?' Walter Mitty took the gun and examined it expertly. 'This is my Webley-Vickers 50.80,' he said calmly. An excited buzz ran around the courtroom. The judge rapped for order. 'You are a crack shot with any sort of firearms, I believe?' said the District Attorney, insinuatingly. 'Objection!' shouted Mitty's attorney. 'We have shown that the defendant could not have fired the shot. We have shown that he

wore his right arm in a sling on the night of the fourteenth of July.'
Walter Mitty raised his hand briefly and the bickering attorneys
were stilled. 'With any known make of gun,' he said evenly, 'I could
have killed Gregory Fitzhurst at three hundred feet *with my left
hand*.' Pandemonium broke loose in the courtroom. A woman's
scream rose above the bedlam and suddenly a lovely, dark-haired
girl was in Walter Mitty's arms. The District Attorney struck at
her savagely. Without rising from his chair, Mitty let the man have
it on the point of the chin. 'You miserable cur!'....

'Puppy biscuit,' said Walter Mitty. He stopped walking and the
buildings of Waterbury rose up out of the misty courtroom and
surrounded him again. A woman who was passing laughed. 'He
said "Puppy biscuit",' she said to her companion. 'That man said
"Puppy biscuit" to himself.' Walter Mitty hurried on. He went
into an A. & P., not the first one he came to but a smaller one
farther up the street. 'I want some biscuit for small, young dogs,'
he said to the clerk. 'Any special brand, sir?' The greatest pistol
shot in the world thought a moment. 'It says "Puppies Bark for
It" on the box,' said Walter Mitty.

His wife would be through at the hairdresser's in fifteen minutes,
Mitty saw in looking at his watch, unless they had trouble drying
it; sometimes they had trouble drying it. She didn't like to get to
the hotel first; she would want him to be there waiting for her as
usual. He found a big leather chair in the lobby, facing a window,
and he put the overshoes and the puppy biscuit on the floor beside
it. He picked up an old copy of *Liberty* and sank down into the
chair. 'Can Germany Conquer the World Through the Air?'
Walter Mitty looked at the pictures of bombing planes and of
ruined streets.

... 'The cannonading has got the wind up in young Raleigh,
sir,' said the sergeant. Captain Mitty looked up at him through
tousled hair. 'Get him to bed,' he said wearily. 'With the others.
I'll fly alone.' 'But you can't, sir,' said the sergeant anxiously. 'It
takes two men to handle that bomber and the Archies are pounding
hell out of the air. Von Richtman's circus is between here and
Saulier.' 'Somebody's got to get that ammunition dump,' said
Mitty. 'I'm going over. Spot of brandy?' He poured a drink for
the sergeant and one for himself. War thundered and whined
around the dugout and battered at the door. There was a rending
of wood and splinters flew through the room. 'A bit of a near thing,'

said Captain Mitty carelessly. 'The box barrage is closing in,' said the sergeant. 'We only live once, Sergeant,' said Mitty, with his faint, fleeting smile. 'Or do we?' He poured another brandy and tossed it off. 'I never see a man could hold his brandy like you, sir,' said the sergeant. 'Begging your pardon, sir.' Captain Mitty stood up and strapped on his huge Webley-Vickers automatic. 'It's forty kilometres through hell, sir,' said the sergeant. Mitty finished one last brandy. 'After all,' he said softly, 'what isn't?' The pounding of the cannon increased; there was the rat-tat-tatting of machine-guns, and from somewhere came the menacing pocketa-pocketa-pocketa of the new flame-throwers. Walter Mitty walked to the door of the dugout humming 'Auprès de Ma Blonde'. He turned and waved to the sergeant. 'Cheerio!' he said. . . .

Something struck his shoulder. 'I've been looking all over this hotel for you,' said Mrs Mitty. 'Why do you have to hide in this old chair? How did you expect me to find you?' 'Things close in,' said Walter Mitty vaguely. 'What?' Mrs Mitty said. 'Did you get the what's-its-name? The puppy biscuit? What's in that box?' 'Overshoes,' said Mitty. 'Couldn't you have put them on in the store?' 'I was thinking,' said Walter Mitty. 'Does it ever occur to you that I am sometimes thinking?' She looked at him. 'I'm going to take your temperature when I get you home,' she said.

They went out through the revolving doors that made a faintly derisive whistling sound when you pushed them. It was two blocks to the parking lot. At the drugstore on the corner she said, 'Wait here for me. I forgot something. I won't be a minute.' She was more than a minute. Walter Mitty lighted a cigarette. It began to rain, rain with sleet in it. He stood up against the wall of the drugstore, smoking. . . . He put his shoulders back and his heels together. 'To hell with the handkerchief,' said Walter Mitty scornfully. He took one last drag on his cigarette and snapped it away. Then, with that faint, fleeting smile playing about his lips, he faced the firing squad; erect and motionless, proud and disdainful, Walter Mitty the Undefeated, inscrutable to the last.

James Thurber

The Macbeth Murder Mystery

'It was a stupid mistake to make,' said the American woman I had met at my hotel in the English lake country, 'but it was on the counter with the other Penguin books—the little sixpenny ones, you know, with the paper covers—and I supposed of course it was a detective story. All the others were detective stories. I'd read all the others, so I bought this one without really looking at it carefully. You can imagine how mad I was when I found it was Shakespeare.' I murmured something sympathetically. 'I don't see why the Penguin-books people had to get out Shakespeare plays in the same size and everything as the detective stories,' went on my companion. 'I think they have different-coloured jackets,' I said. 'Well, I didn't notice that,' she said. 'Anyway, I got real comfy in bed that night and all ready to read a good mystery story and here I had *The Tragedy of Macbeth*—a book for high-school students. 'Like *Ivanhoe* or *Lorna Doone*,' I said. 'Exactly,' said the American lady, 'And I was just crazy for a good Agatha Christie, or something. Hercule Poirot is my favourite detective.' 'Is he the rabbity one?' I asked. 'Oh, no,' said my crime-fiction expert. 'He's the Belgian one. You're thinking of Mr Pinkerton, the one that helps Inspector Bull. He's good, too.'

Over her second cup of tea my companion began to tell the plot of a detective story that had fooled her completely—it seems it was the old family doctor all the time. But I cut in on her. 'Tell me,' I said. 'Did you read *Macbeth*?' 'I *had* to read it,' she said. 'There wasn't a scrap of anything else to read in the whole room.' 'Did you like it?' I asked. 'No, I did not,' she said decisively. 'In the first place, I don't think for a moment that Macbeth did it.' I looked at her blankly. 'Did what?' I asked. 'I don't think for a moment that he killed the King,' she said. 'I don't think the Macbeth woman was mixed up in it, either. You suspect them the most, of course, but those are the ones that are never guilty—or shouldn't be, anyway.' 'I'm afraid,' I began, 'that I—' 'But don't you see?' said the American lady. 'It would spoil everything if you could figure out right away who did it. Shakespeare was too smart for

that. I've read that people never *have* figured out *Hamlet*, so it isn't
likely Shakespeare would have made *Macbeth* as simple as it seems,'
I thought this over while I filled my pipe. 'Who do you suspect?'
I asked, suddenly. 'Macduff,' she said, promptly. 'Good God!' I
whispered, softly.

'Oh Macduff did it, all right,' said the murder specialist.
'Hercule Poirot would have got him easily.' 'How did you figure
it out?' I demanded. 'Well,' she said, 'I didn't right away. At first
I suspected Banquo. And then, of course, he was the second person
killed. That was good right in there, that part. The person you
suspect of the first murder should always be the second victim.'
'Is that so?' I murmured. 'Oh, yes,' said my informant. 'They have
to keep surprising you. Well, after the second murder I didn't know
who the killer was for a while.' 'How about Malcolm and Donal-
bain, the King's sons?' I asked. 'As I remember it, they fled right
after the first murder. That looks suspicious.' 'Too suspicious,' said
the American lady. 'Much too suspicious. When they flee, they're
never guilty. You can count on that.' 'I believe,' I said, 'I'll have
a brandy,' and I summoned the waiter. My companion leaned toward me, her eyes bright, her teacup quivering. 'Do you know who
discovered Duncan's body?' she demanded. I said I was sorry, but
I had forgotten. 'Macduff discovers it,' she said, slipping into the
historical present. 'Then he comes running downstairs and shouts,
"Confusion has broke open the Lord's anointed temple" and
"Sacrilegious murder has made his masterpiece" and on and on
like that.' The good lady tapped me on the knee. 'All that stuff
was rehearsed,' she said. 'You wouldn't say a lot of stuff like that,
offhand, would you—if you had found a body?' She fixed me with
a glittering eye. 'I—' I began. 'You're right!' she said. 'You
wouldn't! Unless you had practised it in advance. "My God,
there's a body in here!" is what an innocent man would say.' She
sat back with a confident glare.

I thought for a while. 'But what do you make of the Third Murderer?' I asked. 'You know, the Third Murderer has puzzled *Macbeth* scholars for three hundred years.' 'That's because they never
thought of Macduff,' said the American lady. 'It was Macduff,
I'm certain. You couldn't have one of the victims murdered by
two ordinary thugs—the murderer always has to be somebody important.' 'But what about the banquet scene?' I asked, after a
moment. 'How do you account for Macbeth's guilty actions there,
when Banquo's ghost came in and sat in his chair?' The lady leaned

forward and tapped me on the knee again. 'There wasn't any ghost,' she said. 'A big, strong man like that doesn't go around see-ing ghosts—especially in a brightly lighted banquet hall with dozens of people around. Macbeth was *shielding somebody*!' 'Who was he shielding?' I asked. 'Mrs Macbeth, of course,' she said. 'He thought she did it and he was going to take the rap himself. The husband always does that when the wife is suspected.' 'But what,' I demanded, 'about the sleepwalking scene, then?' 'The same thing, only the other way around,' said my companion. 'That time *she* was shielding *him*. She wasn't asleep at all. Do you remember where it says, "Enter Lady Macbeth with a taper"?' 'Yes,' I said. 'Well, people who walk in their sleep *never carry lights*!' said my fellow-traveller. 'They have a second sight. Did you ever hear of a sleepwalker carrying a light?' 'No,' I said, 'I never did.' 'Well, then, she wasn't asleep. She was acting guilty to shield Macbeth.' 'I think,' I said, 'I'll have another brandy,' and I called the waiter. When he brought it, I drank it rapidly and rose to go. 'I believe,' I said, 'that you have got hold of something. Would you lend me that *Macbeth*? I'd like to look it over tonight. I don't feel, somehow, as if I'd ever really read it.' 'I'll get it for you,' she said. 'But you'll find that I am right.'

I read the play over carefully that night, and the next morning, after breakfast, I sought out the American woman. She was on the putting green, and I came up behind her silently and took her arm. She gave an exclamation. 'Could I see you alone?' I asked, in a low voice. She nodded cautiously and followed me to a secluded spot. 'You've found out something?' she breathed. 'I've found out,' I said, triumphantly, 'the name of the murderer!' 'You mean it wasn't Macduff?' she said. 'Macduff is as innocent of those murders,' I said, 'as Macbeth and the Macbeth woman.' I opened the copy of the play, which I had with me, and turned to Act II, Scene 2. 'Here,' I said, 'you will see where Lady Macbeth says, "I laid their daggers ready. He could not miss 'em. Had he not resembled my father as he slept, I had done it." Do you see?' 'No,' said the American woman, bluntly, 'I don't.' 'But it's simple!' I exclaimed. 'I wonder I didn't see it years ago. The reason Duncan resembled Lady Macbeth's father as he slept is that *it actually was her father*!' 'Good God!' breathed my companion, softly. 'Lady Macbeth's father killed the King,' I said, 'and, hearing someone coming, thrust the body under the bed and crawled into the bed himself.' 'But,' said the lady, 'you can't have a murderer who only appears in the story once. You can't have that.' 'I know that,' I said, and I turned to Act II, Scene 4. 'It says here, "Enter Ross with an old Man." Now, that old man is never identified and it is my contention he was old Mr Macbeth, whose ambition it was to make his daughter Queen. There you have your motive.' 'But even then,' cried the American lady, 'he's still a minor character!' 'Not,' I said, gleefully, 'when you realize that he was also *one of the weird sisters in disguise*!' 'You mean one of the three witches?' 'Precisely,' I said. 'Listen to this speech of the old man's. "On Tuesday last, a falcon towering in her pride of place, was by a mousing owl hawk'd at and kill'd." Who does that sound like?' 'It sounds like the way the three witches talk,' said my companion, reluctantly. 'Precisely!' I said again. 'Well,' said the American woman, 'maybe you're right, but—' 'I'm sure I am,' I said. 'And do you know what I'm going to do now?' 'No,' she said. 'What?' 'Buy a copy of *Hamlet*,' I said, 'and solve *that*!' My companion's eye brightened. 'Then,' she said, 'you don't think Hamlet did it?' 'I am,' I said, 'absolutely positive he didn't.' 'But who,' she demanded, 'do you suspect?' I looked at her cryptically. 'Everybody,' I said, and disappeared into a small grove of trees as silently as I had come.

Mark Twain

The Stolen White Elephant

The following curious history was related to me by a chance railway acquaintance. He was a gentleman more than seventy years of age, and his thoroughly good and gentle face and earnest and sincere manner imprinted the unmistakable stamp of truth upon every statement which fell from his lips. He said:

You know in what reverence the royal white elephant of Siam is held by the people of that country. You know it is sacred to kings, only kings may possess it, and that it is indeed in a measure even superior to kings, since it receives not merely honour but worship. Very well; five years ago, when the troubles concerning the frontier line arose between Great Britain and Siam, it was presently manifest that Siam had been in the wrong. Therefore every reparation was quickly made, and the British representative stated that he was satisfied and the past should be forgotten. This greatly relieved the King of Siam, and partly as a token of gratitude, but partly also, perhaps, to wipe out any little remaining vestige of unpleasantness which England might feel towards him, he wished to send the Queen a present—the sole sure way of propitiating an enemy, according to Oriental ideas. This present ought not only to be a royal one, but transcendentally royal. Wherefore, what offering could be so meet as that of a white elephant? My position in the Indian civil service was such that I was deemed peculiarly worthy of the honour of conveying the present to Her Majesty. A ship was fitted out for me and my servants and the officers and attendants of the elephant, and in due time I arrived in New York harbour and placed my royal charge in admirable quarters in Jersey City. It was necessary to remain awhile in order to recruit the animal's health before resuming the voyage.

All went well during a fortnight; then my calamities began. The white elephant was stolen! I was called up at dead of night and informed of this fearful misfortune. For some moments I was beside myself with terror and anxiety; I was helpless. Then I grew calmer and collected my faculties. I soon saw my course—for indeed there was but the one course for an intelligent man to pursue. Late as it was, I flew to New York and got a policeman to conduct me to the headquarters of the detective force. Fortunately I arrived in time, though the chief of the force, the celebrated Inspector Blunt, was just on the point of leaving for his home. He was a man of middle size and compact frame, and when he was thinking deeply he had a way of knitting his brows and tapping his forehead reflectively with his finger, which impressed you at once with the conviction that you stood in the presence of a person of no common order. The very sight of him gave me confidence and made me hopeful. I stated my errand. It did not flurry him in the least; it had no more visible effect upon his iron self-possession than if I had told him somebody had stolen my dog. He motioned me to a seat, and said calmly:

'Allow me to think a moment, please.'

So saying, he sat down at his office table and leaned his head upon his hand. Several clerks were at work at the other end of the room; the scratching of their pens was all the sound I heard during the next six or seven minutes. Meantime the inspector sat there, buried in thought. Finally he raised his head, and there was that in the firm lines of his face which showed me that his brain had done its work and his plan was made. Said he—and his voice was low and impressive—

'This is no ordinary case. Every step must be warily taken; each step must be made sure before the next is ventured. And secrecy must be observed—secrecy profound and absolute. Speak to no one about the matter, not even the reporters. I will take care of *them*; I will see that they get only what it may suit my ends to let them know.' He touched a bell; a youth appeared. 'Alaric, tell the reporters to remain for the present.' The boy retired. 'Now let us proceed to business—and systematically. Nothing can be accomplished in this trade of mine without strict and minute method.'

He took a pen and some paper. 'Now. Name of the elephant?'

'Hassan Ben Ali Ben Selim Abdallah Mohammed Moisé Alhammal Jamsetjejeebhoy Dhuleep Sultan Ebu Bhudpoor.'

'Very well. Given name?'

'Jumbo.'

'Very well. Place of birth?'

'The capital city of Siam.'

'Parents living?'

'No, dead.'

'Had they any other issue besides this one?'

'None. He was an only child.'

'Very well. These matters are sufficient under that head. Now please describe the elephant, and leave out no particular, however insignificant—that is, insignificant from *your* point of view. To men in my profession there *are* no insignificant particulars; they do not exist.'

I described, he wrote. When I was done, he said:

'Now listen. If I have made any mistakes, correct me.'

He read as follows:

'Height, 19 feet; length from apex of forehead to insertion of tail, 26 feet; length of trunk, 16 feet; length of tail, 6 feet; total length, including trunk and tail, 48 feet; length of tusks, $9\frac{1}{2}$ feet; ears in keeping with these dimensions; footprint resembles the mark left when one upends a barrel in the snow; colour of the elephant, a dull white; has a hole the size of a plate in each ear for the insertion of jewellery, and possesses the habit in a remarkable degree of squirting water upon spectators and of maltreating with his trunk not only such persons as he is acquainted with, but even entire strangers; limps slightly with his right hind leg, and has a small scar in his left armpit caused by a former boil; had on, when stolen, a castle containing seats for fifteen persons, and a gold-cloth saddle-blanket the size of an ordinary carpet.'

There were no mistakes. The inspector touched the bell, handed the description to Alaric, and said:

'Have fifty thousand copies of this printed at once and mailed to every detective office and pawnbroker's shop on the continent.' Alaric retired. 'There—so far, so good. Next, I must have a photograph of the property.'

I gave him one. He examined it critically, and said:

'It must do, since we can do no better; but he has his trunk curled up and tucked into his mouth. That is unfortunate, and is calculated to mislead, for of course he does not usually have it in that position.' He touched his bell.

'Alaric, have fifty thousand copies of this photograph made, the first thing in the morning, and mail them with the descriptive circulars.'

Alaric retired to execute his orders. The inspector said:

'It will be necessary to offer a reward, of course. Now as to the amount?'

'What sum would you suggest?'

'To *begin* with, I should say, well, twenty-five thousand dollars. It is an intricate and difficult business; there are a thousand avenues of escape and opportunities of concealment. These thieves have friends and pals everywhere—'

'Bless me, do you know who they are?'

The wary face, practised in concealing the thoughts and feelings within, gave me no token, nor yet the replying words, so quietly uttered.

'Never mind about that. I may, and I may not. We generally gather a pretty shrewd inkling of who our man is by the manner of his work and the size of the game he goes after. We are not dealing with a pickpocket or a hall thief, now, make up your mind to that. This property was not "lifted" by a novice. But, as I was saying, considering the amount of travel which will have to be done, and the diligence with which the thieves will cover up their traces as they move along, twenty-five thousand may be too small a sum to offer, yet I think it worth while to start with that.'

So we determined upon that figure, as a beginning. Then this man, whom nothing escaped which could by any possibility be made to serve as a clue, said:

'There are cases in detective history to show that criminals have been detected through peculiarities in their appetites. Now, what does this elephant eat, and how much?'

'Well, as to *what* he eats, he will eat *anything*. He will eat a man, he will eat a Bible, he will eat anything *between* a man and a Bible.'

'Good, very good indeed, but too general. Details are necessary, details are the only valuable things in our trade. Very well—as to men. At one meal—or, if you prefer, during one day—how many men will he eat, if fresh?'

'He would not care whether they were fresh or not; at a single meal he would eat five ordinary men.'

'Very good; five men; we will put that down. What nationalities would he prefer?'

'He is indifferent about nationalities. He prefers acquaintances, but is not prejudiced against strangers.'

'Very good. Now, as to Bibles. How many Bibles would he eat at a meal?'

'He would eat an entire edition.'

'It is hardly succinct enough. Do you mean the ordinary octavo, or the family illustrated?'

'I think he would be indifferent to illustrations; that is, I think he would not value illustrations above simple letterpress.'

'No, you do not get my idea. I refer to bulk. The ordinary octavo Bible weighs about two pounds and a half, while the great quarto with the illustrations weighs ten or twelve. How many Doré Bibles would he eat at a meal?'

'If you knew this elephant, you could not ask. He would take what they had.'

'Well, put it in dollars and cents, then. We must get at it somehow. The Doré costs a hundred dollars a copy, Russia leather, bevelled.'

'He would require about fifty thousand dollars' worth—say an edition of five hundred copies.'

'Now that is more exact. I will put that down. Very well; he likes men and Bibles; so far, so good. What else will he eat? I want particulars.'

'He will leave Bibles to eat bricks, he will leave bricks to eat bottles, he will leave bottles to eat clothing, he will leave clothing to eat cats, he will leave cats to eat oysters, he will leave oysters to eat ham, he will leave ham to eat sugar, he will leave sugar to eat pie, he will leave pie to eat potatoes, he will leave potatoes to eat bran, he will leave bran to eat hay, he will leave hay to eat oats, he will leave oats to eat rice, for he was mainly raised on it. There is nothing whatever that he will not eat but European butter, and he would eat that if he could taste it.'

'Very good. General quantity at a meal—say about—'

'Well, anywhere from a quarter to half a ton.'

'And he drinks—'

'Everything that is fluid. Milk, water, whisky, molasses, castor oil, camphene, carbolic acid—it is no use to go into particulars; whatever fluid occurs to you set it down. He will drink anything that is fluid, except European coffee.'

'Very good. As to quantity?'

'Put it down five to fifteen barrels—his thirst varies; his other appetites do not.'

'These things are unusual. They ought to furnish quite good clues toward tracing him.'

He touched the bell.

'Alaric, summon Captain Burns.'

Burns appeared. Inspector Blunt unfolded the whole matter to him, detail by detail. Then he said in the clear, decisive tones of a man whose plans are clearly defined in his head, and who is accustomed to command:

'Captain Burns, detail Detectives Jones, Davis, Halsey, Bates, and Hackett to shadow the elephant.'

'Yes, sir.'

'Detail Detectives Moses, Dakin, Murphy, Rogers, Tupper, Higgins, and Bartholomew to shadow the thieves.'

'Yes, sir.'

'Place a strong guard—a guard of thirty picked men, with a relief of thirty—over the place from where the elephant was stolen, to keep strict watch there night and day, and allow none to approach—except reporters—without written authority from me.'

'Yes, sir.'

'Place detectives in plain clothes in the railway, steamship, and ferry depots, and upon all roadways leading out of Jersey City, with orders to search all suspicious persons.'

'Yes, sir.'

'Furnish all these men with photograph and accompanying descriptions of the elephant, and instruct them to search all trains and outgoing ferryboats and other vessels.'

'Yes, sir.'

'If the elephant should be found, let him be seized and the information forwarded to me by telegraph.'

'Yes, sir.'

'Let me be informed at once if any clues should be found—footprints of the animal, or anything of that kind.'

'Yes, sir.'

'Get an order commanding the harbour police to patrol the frontages vigilantly.'

'Yes, sir.'

'Despatch detectives in plain clothes over all the railways, north as far as Canada, west as far as Ohio, south as far as Washington.'

'Yes, sir.'

'Place experts in all the telegraph offices to listen to all messages; and let them require that all cipher despatches be interpreted to them.'

'Yes, sir.'

'Let all these things be done with the utmost secrecy—mind, the most impenetrable secrecy.'

'Yes, sir.'

'Report to me promptly at the usual hour.'

'Yes, sir.'

'Go!'

'Yes, sir.'

He was gone.

Inspector Blunt was silent and thoughtful a moment, while the fire in his eye cooled down and faded out. Then he turned to me and said in a placid voice:

'I am not given to boasting, it is not my habit; but—we shall find the elephant.'

I shook him warmly by the hand and thanked him; and I *felt* my thanks, too. The more I had seen of the man the more I liked him, and the more I admired him and marvelled over the mysterious wonders of his profession. Then we parted for the night, and I went home with a far happier heart than I had carried with me to his office.

Next morning it was all in the newspapers, in the minutest detail. It even had additions—consisting of Detective This, Detective That, and Detective The Other's 'Theory' as to how the robbery was done, who the robbers were, and whither they had flown with their booty. There were eleven of these theories, and they covered all the possibilities; and this single fact shows what independent thinkers detectives are. No two theories were alike, or even much resembled each other, save in one striking particular, and in that one all the eleven theories were absolutely agreed. That was, that although the rear of my building was torn out and the only door remained locked, the elephant had not been removed through the rent, but by some other (undiscovered) outlet. All agreed that the robbers had made that rent only to mislead the detectives. That never would have occurred to me or to any other layman, perhaps, but it had not deceived the detectives for a moment. Thus, what I had supposed was the only thing that had no mystery about it was in fact the very thing I had gone furthest astray in. The eleven theories all named the supposed robbers, but no two named the same robbers; the total number of suspected persons was thirty-seven. The various newspaper accounts all closed with the most important opinion of all—that of Chief Inspector Blunt. A portion of this statement read as follows:

'The chief knows who the two principals are, namely, "Brick" Duffy and "Red" McFadden. Ten days before the robbery was achieved he was already aware that it was to be attempted, and had quietly proceeded to shadow these two noted villains; but unfortunately on the night in question their track was lost, and before it could be found again the bird was flown—that is, the elephant.

'Duffy and McFadden are the boldest scoundrels in the profession; the chief has reasons for believing that they are the men who stole the stove out of the detective headquarters on a bitter night last winter—in consequence of which the chief and every detective present were in the hands of the physicians before morning, some with frozen feet, others with frozen fingers, ears, and other members.'

When I read the first half of that I was more astonished than ever at the wonderful sagacity of this strange man. He not only saw everything in the present with a clear eye, but even the future could not be hidden from him. I was soon at his office, and said I could not help wishing he had had those men arrested, and so prevented the trouble and loss; but his reply was simple and unanswerable.

'It is not our province to prevent crime, but to punish it. We cannot punish it until it is committed.'

I remarked that the secrecy with which we had begun had been marred by the newspapers; not only all our facts but all our plans and purposes had been revealed; even all the suspected persons had been named; these would doubtless disguise themselves now, or go into hiding.

'Let them. They will find that when I am ready for them my hand will descend upon them, in their secret places, as unerringly as the hand of fate. As to the newspapers, we *must* keep in with them. Fame, reputation, constant public mention—these are the detective's bread and butter. He must publish his facts, else he will be supposed to have none; he must publish his theory, for nothing is so strange or striking as a detective's theory, or brings him so much wondering respect; we must publish our plans, for these the journals insist upon having, and we could not deny them without offending. We must constantly show the public what we are doing, or they will believe we are doing nothing. It is much pleasanter to have a newspaper say, "Inspector Blunt's ingenious and extraordinary theory is as follows," than to have it say some harsh thing, or, worse still, some sarcastic one.'

'I see the force of what you say. But I noticed that in one part of your remarks in the papers this morning you refused to reveal your opinion upon a certain minor point.'

'Yes, we always do that; it has a good effect. Besides, I had not formed any opinion on that point, anyway.'

I deposited a considerable sum of money with the inspector, to meet current expenses, and sat down to wait for news. We were expecting the telegrams to begin to arrive at any moment now. Meantime I re-read the newspapers and also our descriptive circular, and observed that our $25,000 reward seemed to be offered only to detectives. I said I thought it ought to be offered to anybody who would catch the elephant. The inspector said:

'It is the detectives who will find the elephant, hence the reward will go to the right place. If other people found the animal, it would only be by watching the detectives and taking advantage of clues and indications stolen from them, and that would entitle the detectives to the reward, after all. The proper office of a reward is to stimulate the men who deliver up their time and their trained sagacities to this sort of work, and not to confer benefits upon chance citizens who stumble upon a capture without having earned the benefits by their own merits and labours.'

This was reasonable enough, certainly. Now the telegraphic machine in the corner began to click and the following despatch was the result:

> FLOWER STATION, N.Y., 7:30 A.M.
> Have got a clue. Found a succession of deep tracks across a farm near here. Followed them two miles east without result; think elephant went west. Shall now shadow him in that direction.
>
> DARLEY, *Detective.*

'Darley's one of the best men on the force,' said the inspector. 'We shall hear from him again before long.'

Telegram No. 2 came:

> BARKER'S, N.J., 7:40 A.M.
> Just arrived. Glass factory broken open here during night, and eight hundred bottles taken. Only water in large quantity near here is five miles distant. Shall strike for there. Elephant will be thirsty. Bottles were empty.
>
> BAKER, *Detective.*

'That promises well, too,' said the inspector. 'I told you the creature's appetites would not be bad clues.' Telegram No. 3:

> TAYLORVILLE, L.I., 8:15 A.M.
> A haystack near here disappeared during night. Probably eaten. Have got a clue, and am off.
>
> HUBBARD, *Detective.*

'How he does move around!' said the inspector. 'I knew we had a difficult job on hand, but we shall catch him yet.'

FLOWER STATION, N.Y., 9 A.M.

Shadowed the tracks three miles westward. Large, deep, and ragged. Have just met a farmer who says they are not elephant tracks. Says they are holes where he dug up saplings for shade trees when ground was frozen last winter. Give me orders how to proceed.

DARLEY, *Detective.*

'Aha! a confederate of the thieves! The thing grows warm,' said the inspector.

He dictated the following telegram to Darley:

Arrest the man and force him to name his pals. Continue to follow the tracks—to the Pacific, if necessary.

Chief BLUNT.

Next telegram:

CONEY POINT, PA., 8:45 A.M.

Gas office broken open here during night and three months' unpaid gas bills taken. Have got a clue and am away.

MURPHY, *Detective.*

'Heavens!' said the inspector; 'would he eat gas bills?'

'Through ignorance, yes; but they cannot support life. At least, unassisted.'

Now came this exciting telegram:

IRONVILLE, N.Y., 9:30 A.M.

Just arrived. This village in consternation. Elephant passed through here at five this morning. Some say he went east, some say west, some north, some south—but all say they did not wait to notice particularly. He killed a horse; have secured a piece of it for a clue. Killed it with his trunk; from style of blow, think he struck it left-handed. From position in which horse lies, think elephant travelled northward along line of Berkley railway. Has four and half hours' start, but I move on his track at once.

HAWES, *Detective.*

I uttered exclamations of joy. The inspector was as self-contained as a graven image. He calmly touched his bell.

'Alaric, send Captain Burns here.'

Burns appeared.

'How many men are ready for instant orders?'

'Ninety-six, sir.'

'Send them north at once. Let them concentrate along the line of the Berkley road north of Ironville.'

'Yes, sir.'

'Let them conduct their movements with the utmost secrecy. As fast as others are at liberty, hold them for orders.'

'Yes, sir.'

'Go!'

'Yes, sir.'

Presently came another telegram:

SAGE CORNERS, N.Y., 10:30.

Just arrived. Elephant passed through here at 8:15. All escaped from the town but a policeman. Apparently elephant did not strike at policeman, but at the lamppost. Got both. I have secured a portion of the policeman as clue.

STUMM, *Detective.*

'So the elephant has turned westward,' said the inspector. 'However, he will not escape, for my men are scattered all over that region.'

The next telegram said:

GLOVER'S, 11:15.

Just arrived. Village deserted, except sick and aged. Elephant passed through three quarters of an hour ago. The anti-temperance mass meeting was in session; he put his truck in at a window and washed it out with water from cistern. Some swallowed it—since dead; several drowned. Detectives Cross and O'Shaughnessy were passing through town, but going south—so missed elephant. Whole region for many miles around in terror—people flying from their homes. Wherever they turn they meet elephant, and many are killed.

BRANT, *Detective.*

I could have shed tears, this havoc so distressed me. But the inspector only said:

'You see—we are closing in on him. He feels our presence; he has turned eastward again.'

Yet further troublous news was in store for us. The telegraph brought this:

HOGANPORT, 12:19.

Just arrived. Elephant passed through half an hour ago, creating wildest fright and excitement. Elephant raged around streets; two plumbers going by, killed one—other escaped. Regret general.

O'FLAHERTY, *Detective.*

'Now he is right in the midst of my men,' said the inspector. 'Nothing can save him.'

A succession of telegrams came from detectives who were scattered through New Jersey and Pennsylvania, and who were following clues consisting of ravaged barns, factories, and Sunday school libraries, with high hopes—hopes amounting to certainties, indeed. The inspector said:

'I wish I could communicate with them and order them north, but that is impossible. A detective only visits a telegraph office to send his report; then he is off again, and you don't know where to put your hand on him.'

Now came this despatch:

BRIDGEPORT, CT., 12:15.

Barnum offers rate of $4,000 a year for exclusive privilege of using elephant as travelling advertising medium from now till detectives find him. Wants to paste circus posters on him. Desires immediate answer.

BOGGS, *Detective.*

'That is perfectly absurd!' I exclaimed.

'Of course it is,' said the inspector. 'Evidently Mr Barnum, who thinks he is so sharp, does not know me—but I know him.'

Then he dictated this answer to the despatch:

Mr Barnum's offer declined. Make it $7,000 or nothing.

Chief BLUNT.

'There. We shall not have to wait long for an answer. Mr Barnum is not at home; he is in the telegraph office—it is his way when he has business on hand. Inside of three—'

DONE.—P. T. BARNUM.

So interrupted the clicking telegraphic instrument. Before I could make a comment upon this extraordinary episode, the following despatch carried my thoughts into another and very distressing channel:

BOLIVIA, N.Y., 12:50.

Elephant arrived here from the south and passed through toward the forest at 11:50, dispersing a funeral on the way, and diminishing the mourners by two. Citizens fired some small cannon balls into him, and then fled. Detective Burke and I arrived ten minutes later, from the north, but mistook some excavations for footprints, and so lost a good deal of time; but at last we struck the right trail and followed it to the woods. We then got down on our hands and knees and continued to keep a sharp eye on the track, and so shadowed it into the brush. Burke was in advance. Unfortunately the animal had stopped to rest; therefore, Burke having his head down, intent upon the track, butted up against the elephant's hind legs before he was aware of his vicinity. Burke instantly rose to his feet, seized the tail, and exclaimed joyfully, 'I claim the re—' but got no further, for a single blow of the huge trunk laid the brave fellow's fragments low in death. I fled rearward, and the elephant turned and shadowed me to the edge of the wood, making tremendous speed, and I should inevitably have been lost, but that the remains of the funeral providentially intervened again and diverted his attention. I have just learned that nothing of that funeral is now left; but this is no loss, for there is an abundance of material for another. Meantime, the elephant has disappeared again.

MULROONEY, *Detective.*

We heard no news except from the diligent and confident detectives scattered about New Jersey, Pennsylvania, Delaware, and Virginia—who were all following fresh and encouraging clues—until shortly after 2 P.M., when this telegram came:

BAXTER CENTER, 2:15.

Elephant been here, plastered over with circus bills, and broke up a revival, striking down and damaging many who were on the point of entering upon a better life. Citizens penned him up, and established a guard. When Detective Brown and I arrived, some time after, we entered enclosure and proceeded to identify elephant by photograph and description. All marks tallied exactly except one, which we could not see—the boil-scar under armpit. To make sure, Brown crept under to look, and was immediately brained—that is, head crushed and destroyed, though nothing issued from debris. All fled; so did elephant, striking right and left with much effect. Has escaped, but left bold blood track from cannon-wounds. Rediscovery certain. He broke southward, through a dense forest.

BRENT, *Detective.*

That was the last telegram. At nightfall a fog shut down which was so dense that objects but three feet away could not be discerned. This lasted all night. The ferry boats and even the omnibuses had to stop running.

Next morning the papers were as full of detective theories as before; they had all our tragic facts in detail also, and a great many more which they had received from their telegraphic correspondents. Column after column was occupied, a third of its way down, with glaring headlines, which it made my heart sick to read. Their general tone was like this:

'THE WHITE ELEPHANT AT LARGE! HE MOVES UPON HIS FATAL MARCH! WHOLE VILLAGES DESERTED BY THEIR FRIGHT-STRICKEN OCCUPANTS! PALE TERROR GOES BEFORE HIM, DEATH AND DEVASTATION FOLLOW AFTER! AFTER THESE, THE DETECTIVES. BARNS DESTROYED, FACTORIES GUTTED, HARVESTS DEVOURED, PUBLIC ASSEMBLAGES DISPERSED, ACCOMPANIED BY SCENES OF CARNAGE IMPOSSIBLE TO DESCRIBE! THEORIES OF THIRTY-FOUR OF THE MOST DISTINGUISHED DETECTIVES ON THE FORCE! THEORY OF CHIEF BLUNT!'

'There!' said Inspector Blunt, almost betrayed into excitement, 'this is magnificent! This is the greatest windfall that any detective organization ever had. The fame of it will travel to the ends of the earth, and endure to the end of time, and my name with it.'

But there was no joy for me. I felt as if I had committed all those red crimes, and that the elephant was only my irresponsible agent. And how the list had grown! In one place he had 'interfered with an election and killed five repeaters'. He had followed this act with the destruction of two poor fellows, named O'Donohue and McFlannigan, who had 'found a refuge in the home of the oppressed of all lands only the day before, and were in the act of exercising for the first time the noble right of American citizens at the polls, when stricken down by the relentless hand of the Scourge of Siam'. In another, he had 'found a crazy sensation-preacher preparing his next season's heroic attack on the dance, the theatre, and other things which can't strike back, and had stepped on him'. And in still another place he had 'killed a lightning-rod agent'. And so the list went on, growing redder and redder, and more and more heartbreaking. Sixty persons had been killed, and two hundred and forty wounded. All the accounts bore just testimony to the activity and devotion of the detectives, and all closed with the remark that 'three hundred thousand citizens and four detectives saw the dread creature, and two of the latter he destroyed'.

I dreaded to hear the telegraphic instrument begin to click again. By and by the messages began to pour in, but I was happily disappointed in their nature. It was soon apparent that all trace of the elephant was lost. The fog had enabled him to search out a good hiding place unobserved. Telegrams from the most absurdly distant points reported that a dim vast mass had been glimpsed there through the fog at such and such an hour, and was 'undoubtedly the elephant'. This dim vast mass had been glimpsed in New Haven, in New Jersey, in Pennsylvania, in interior New York, in Brooklyn, and even in the city of New York itself! But in all cases the dim vast mass had vanished quickly and left no trace. Every detective of the large force scattered over this huge extent of country sent his hourly report, and each and every one of them had a clue, and was shadowing something, and was hot upon the heels of it.

But the day passed without other result.

The next day the same.

The next just the same.

The newspaper reports began to grow monotonous with facts that amounted to nothing, clues which led to nothing, and theories which had nearly exhausted the elements which surprise and delight and dazzle.

By advice of the inspector I doubled the reward.

Four more dull days followed. Then came a bitter blow to the poor, hard-working detectives—the journalists declined to print their theories, and coldly said, 'Give us a rest.'

Two weeks after the elephant's disappearance I raised the reward to $75,000 by the inspector's advice. It was a great sum, but I felt that I would rather sacrifice my whole private fortune than lose my credit with my government. Now that the detectives were in adversity, the newspapers turned upon them, and began to fling the most stinging sarcasms at them. This gave the minstrels an idea, and they dressed themselves as detectives and hunted the elephant on the stage in the most extravagant way. The caricaturists made pictures of detectives scanning the country with spyglasses, while the elephant, at their backs, stole apples out of their pockets. And they made all sorts of ridiculous pictures of the detective badge— you have seen that badge printed in gold on the back of detective novels, no doubt—it is a wide-staring eye, with the legend, 'WE NEVER SLEEP.' When detectives called for a drink, the would-be facetious barkeeper resurrected an obsolete form of expression and said, 'Will you have an eye-opener?' All the air was thick with sarcasms.

But there was one man who moved calm, untouched, unaffected, through it all. It was that heart of oak, the Chief Inspector. His brave eye never drooped, his serene confidence never wavered. He always said:

'Let them rail on; he laughs best who laughs last.'

My admiration for the man grew into a species of worship. I was at his side always. His office had become an unpleasant place to me, and now became daily more and more so. Yet if he could endure it I meant to do so also; at least, as long as I could. So I came regularly, and stayed—the only outsider who seemed to be capable of it. Everybody wondered how I could; and often it seemed to me that I must desert, but at such times I looked into that calm and apparently unconscious face, and held my ground.

About three weeks after the elephant's disappearance I was about to say, one morning, that I should *have* to strike my colours and retire, when the great detective arrested the thought by proposing one more superb and masterly move.

This was to compromise with the robbers. The fertility of this man's invention exceeded anything I have ever seen, and I have had a wide intercourse with the world's finest minds. He said he was confident he could compromise for $100,000 and recover the elephant. I said I believed I could scrape the amount together, but what would become of the poor detectives who had worked so faithfully? He said:

'In compromises they always get half.'

This removed my only objection. So the inspector wrote two notes, in this form:

> DEAR MADAM—Your husband can make a large sum of money (and be entirely protected from the law) by making an immediate appointment with me.
>
> *Chief* BLUNT.

He sent one of these by his confidential messenger to the 'reputed wife' of Brick Duffy, and the other to the 'reputed wife' of Red McFadden.

Within the hour these offensive answers came:

> YE OWLD FOOL: brick McDuffey's bin ded 2 yere.
>
> BRIDGET MAHONEY.

> CHIEF BAT—Red McFadden is hung and in heving 18 month. Any Ass but a detective knose that.
>
> MARY O'HOOLIGAN.

'I had long suspected these facts,' said the inspector; 'this testimony proves the unerring accuracy of my instinct.'

The moment one resource failed him he was ready with another.

He immediately wrote an advertisement for the morning papers, and I kept a copy of it.

A.—xwblv. 242 N. Tjnd—fz328wmlg. Ozpo—; 2 mo. ogw. Mum.

He said that if the thief was alive this would bring him to the usual rendezvous. He further explained that the usual rendezvous was a place where all business affairs between detectives and criminals were conducted. This meeting would take place at twelve the next night.

We could do nothing till then, and I lost no time in getting out of the office, and was grateful indeed for the privilege.

At 11 the next night I brought $100,000 in banknotes and put them into the chief's hands, and shortly afterward he took his leave, with the brave old undimmed confidence in his eye. An almost intolerable hour dragged to a close; then I heard his welcome tread, and rose gasping and tottered to meet him. How his fine eyes flamed with triumph! He said:

'We've compromised! The jokers will sing a different tune tomorrow! Follow me!'

He took a lighted candle and strode down into the vast vaulted basement where sixty detectives always slept, and where a score were now playing cards to while the time. I followed close after him. He walked swiftly down to the dim remote end of the place, and just as I succumbed to the pangs of suffocation and was swooning away he stumbled and fell over the outlying members of a mighty object, and I heard him exclaim as he went down:

'Our noble profession is vindicated. Here is your elephant!'

I was carried to the office above and restored with carbolic acid. The whole detective force swarmed in, and such another season of triumphant rejoicing ensued as I had never witnessed before. The reporters were called, baskets of champagne were opened, toasts were drunk, the handshakings and congratulations were continuous and enthusiastic. Naturally the chief was the hero of the hour, and his happiness was so complete and had been so patiently and worthily and bravely won that it made me happy to see it, though I stood there a homeless beggar, my priceless charge dead, and my position in my country's service lost to me through what would always seem my fatally careless execution of a great trust. Many an eloquent eye testified its deep admiration for the chief, and many a detective's voice murmured, 'Look at him—just the king of the profession—only give him a clue, it's all he wants, and there ain't anything hid that he can't find.' The dividing of the $50,000 made great pleasure; when it was finished the chief made a little speech while he put his share in his pocket, in which he said, 'Enjoy it, boys, for you've earned it; and more than that you've earned for the detective profession undying fame.'

A telegram arrived, which read:

> MONROE, MICH., 10 P.M.
>
> First time I've struck a telegraph office in over three weeks. Have followed those footprints, horseback, through the woods, a thousand miles to here, and they get stronger and bigger and fresher every day. Don't worry—inside of another week I'll have the elephant. This is dead sure.
>
> DARLEY, *Detective.*

The chief ordered three cheers for 'Darley, one of the finest minds on the force', and then commanded that he be telegraphed to come home and receive his share of the reward.

So ended that marvellous episode of the stolen elephant. The newspapers were pleasant with praises once more, the next day, with one contemptible exception. This sheet said, 'Great is the detective! He may be a little slow in finding a little thing like a mislaid elephant—he may hunt him all day and sleep with his rotting carcass all night for three weeks, but he will find him at last—if he can get the man who mislaid him to show him the place!'

Poor Hassan was lost to me forever. The cannon shots had wounded him fatally, he had crept to that unfriendly place in the fog, and there, surrounded by his enemies and in constant danger of detection, he had wasted away with hunger and suffering till death gave him peace.

The compromise cost me $100,000; my detective expenses were $42,000 more; I never applied for a place again under my government; I am a ruined man and a wanderer in the earth—but my admiration for that man, whom I believe to be the greatest detective the world has ever produced, remains undimmed to this day, and will so remain unto the end.

H. G. Wells

The Truth about Pyecraft

He sits not a dozen yards away. If I glance over my shoulder I can see him. And if I catch his eye—and usually I catch his eye, it meets me with an expression—

It is mainly an imploring look—and yet with suspicion in it.

Confound his suspicion! If I wanted to tell on him I should have told long ago. I don't tell and I won't tell, and he ought to feel at his ease. As if anything so gross and fat as he could feel at ease! Who would believe it if I did tell?

Poor old Pyecraft! Great, uneasy jelly of substance! The fattest clubman in London.

He sits at one of the little club tables in the huge bay by the fire, stuffing. What is he stuffing? I glance judiciously and catch him biting at a round of hot buttered teacake, with his eyes on me. Confound him!—with his eyes on me!

That settles it, Pyecraft. Since you *will* be abject, since you *will* behave as though I was not a man of honour, here, right under your embedded eyes, I write the thing down—the plain truth about Pyecraft. The man I helped, the man I shielded, and who has requited me by making my club unendurable, absolutely unendurable, with his liquid appeal, with the perpetual 'don't tell' of his looks.

And besides, why does he keep on eternally eating?

Well, here goes for the truth, the whole truth, and nothing but the truth!

Pyecraft—I made the acquaintance of Pyecraft in this very smoking-room. I was a young, nervous new member, and he saw it. I was sitting all alone, wishing I knew more of the members, and suddenly he came, a great rolling front of chins and abdomina, towards me, and grunted and sat down in a chair close by me, and wheezed for a space, and scraped for a space with a match and lit a cigar, and then addressed me. I forget what he said— something about the matches not lighting properly, and afterwards as he talked he kept stopping the waiters one by one as they went by, and telling them about the matches in that thin, fluty voice he has. But, anyhow, it was in some such way we began our talking.

He talked about various things and came round to games. And thence to my figure and complexion. 'You ought to be a good cricketer,' he said. I suppose I am slender, slender to what some people would call lean, and I suppose I am rather dark still—I am not ashamed of having a Hindu great-grandmother, but, for all that, I don't want casual strangers to see through me at a glance to *her*. So that I was set against Pyecraft from the beginning.

But he only talked about me in order to get to himself.

'I expect,' he said, 'you take no more exercise than I do, and probably eat no less.' (Like all excessively obese people he fancied he ate nothing.) 'Yet'—and he smiled an oblique smile—'we differ.'

And then he began to talk about his fatness and his fatness; all he did for his fatness and all he was going to do for his fatness; what people had advised him to do for his fatness and what he had heard of people doing for fatness similar to his. '*A priori*,' he said, 'one would think a question of nutrition could be answered by dietary and a question of assimilation by drugs.' It was stifling. It was dumpling talk. It made me feel swelled to hear him.

One stands that sort of thing once in a way at a club, but a time came when I fancied I was standing too much. He took to me altogether too conspicuously. I could never go into the smoking-room but he would come wallowing towards me, and sometimes he came and gormandized round and about me while I had my lunch. He seemed at times almost to be clinging to me. He was a bore, but not so fearful a bore as to be limited to me; and from the first there was something in his manner—almost as though he knew, almost as though he penetrated to the fact that I *might*—that there was a remote, exceptional chance in me that no one else presented.

'I'd give anything to get it down,' he would say—'anything,' and peer at me over his vast cheeks and pant.

Poor old Pyecraft! He has just gonged, no doubt to order another buttered teacake!

He came to the actual thing one day. 'Our Pharmacopoeia,' he said, 'our Western Pharmacopoeia is anything but the last word of medical science. In the East, I've been told—'

He stopped and stared at me. It was like being at an aquarium.

I was quite suddenly angry with him. 'Look here,' I said, 'who told you about my great-grandmother's recipes?'

'Well?' he fenced.

'Every time we've met for a week,' I said—'and we've met pretty often—you've given me a broad hint or so about that little secret of mine.'

'Well,' he said, 'now the cat's out of the bag, I'll admit, yes, it is so. I had it—'

'From Pattison?'

'Indirectly,' he said, which I believe was lying, 'yes.'

'Pattison,' I said, 'took that stuff at his own risk.'

He pursed his mouth and bowed.

'My great-grandmother's recipes,' I said, 'are queer things to handle. My father was near making me promise—'

'He didn't?'

'No. But he warned me. He himself used one—once.'

'Ah! ... But do you think—? Suppose—suppose there did happen to be one—'

'The things are curious documents,' I said. 'Even the smell of 'em.... No!'

But after going so far Pyecraft was resolved I should go farther. I was always a little afraid if I tried his patience too much he would fall on me suddenly and smother me. I own I was weak. But I was also annoyed with Pyecraft. I had got to that state of feeling for him that disposed me to say, 'Well, *take* the risk!' The little affair of Pattison to which I have alluded was a different matter altogether. What it was doesn't concern us now, but I knew, anyhow, that the particular recipe I used then was safe. The rest I didn't know so much about, and, on the whole, I was inclined to doubt their safety pretty completely.

Yet even if Pyecraft got poisoned—

I must confess the poisoning of Pyecraft struck me as an immense undertaking.

That evening I took that queer, odd-scented sandalwood box out of my safe and turned the rustling skins over. The gentleman who wrote the recipes for my great-grandmother evidently had a weakness for skins of a miscellaneous origin, and his handwriting was cramped to the last degree. Some of the things are quite unreadable to me—though my family, with its Indian Civil Service associations, has kept up a knowledge of Hindustani from generation to generation—and none are absolutely plain sailing. But I found the one that I knew was there soon enough, and sat on the floor by my safe for some time looking at it.

'Look here,' said I to Pyecraft next day, and snatched the slip away from his eager grasp.

'So far as I can make it out, this is a recipe for Loss of Weight. ('Ah!' said Pyecraft.) I'm not absolutely sure, but I think it's that. And if you take my advice you'll leave it alone. Because, you know—I blacken my blood in your interest, Pyecraft—my ancestors on that side were, so far as I can gather, a jolly queer lot. See?'

'Let me try it,' said Pyecraft.

I leant back in my chair. My imagination made one mighty effort and fell flat within me. 'What in Heaven's name, Pyecraft,' I asked, 'do you think you'll look like when you get thin?'

He was impervious to reason. I made him promise never to say a word to me about his disgusting fatness again, whatever happened—never, and then I handed him that little piece of skin.

'It's nasty stuff,' I said.

'No matter,' he said, and took it.

He goggled at it. 'But—but—' he said.

He had just discovered that it wasn't English.

'To the best of my ability,' I said, 'I will do you a translation.' I did my best. After that we didn't speak for a fortnight. Whenever he approached me I frowned and motioned him away, and he respected our compact, but at the end of the fortnight he was as fat as ever. And then he got a word in.

'I must speak,' he said. 'It isn't fair. There's something wrong. It's done me no good. You're not doing your great-grandmother justice.'

'Where's the recipe?'

He produced it gingerly from his pocket-book.

I ran my eye over the items. 'Was the egg addled?' I asked him.

'No. Ought it to have been?'

'That,' I said, 'goes without saying in all my poor dear great-grandmother's recipes. When condition or quality is not specified you must get the worst. She was drastic or nothing. . . . And there's one or two possible alternatives to some of these other things. You got *fresh* rattlesnake venon?'

'I got rattlesnake from Jamrach's. It cost—it cost—'

'That's your affair, anyhow. This last item—'

'I know a man who—'

'Yes. H'm. Well, I'll write the alternatives down. So far as I know the language, the spelling of this recipe is particularly atrocious. By-the-by, dog here probably means pariah dog.'

For a month after that I saw Pyecraft constantly at the club and as fat and anxious as ever. He kept our treaty, but at times he broke the spirit of it by shaking his head despondently. Then one day in the cloak-room he said, 'Your great-grandmother—'

'Not a word against her,' I said; and he held his peace.

I could have fancied he had desisted, and I saw him one day talking to three new members about his fatness as though he was in search of other recipes. And then, quite unexpectedly his telegram came.

'Mr Formalyn!' bawled a page-boy under my nose and I took the telegram and opened it at once.

'*For Heaven's sake come.—Pyecraft.*'

'H'm,' said I, and to tell the truth I was so pleased at the rehabilitation of my great-grandmother's reputation this evidently promised that I made a most excellent lunch.

I got Pyecraft's address from the hall porter. Pyecraft inhabited the upper half of a house in Bloomsbury, and I went there as soon as I had done my coffee and Trappistine. I did not wait to finish my cigar.

'Mr Pyecraft—?' said I, at the front door.

They believed he was ill; he hadn't been out for two days.

'He expects me,' said I, and they sent me up.

I rang the bell at the lattice-door upon the landing.

'He shouldn't have tried it, anyhow,' I said to myself. 'A man who eats like a pig ought to look like a pig.'

An obviously worthy woman, with an anxious face and carelessly placed cap, came and surveyed me through the lattice.

I gave my name and she opened his door for me in a dubious fashion.

'Well?' said I, as we stood together inside Pyecraft's piece of the landing.

' 'E said you was to come in if you came,' she said, and regarded me, making no motion to show me anywhere. And then, confidentially, ' 'E's locked in, sir.'

'Locked in?'

'Locked himself in yesterday morning and 'asn't let anyone in since, sir. And ever and again *swearing*. Oh, my!'

I stared at the door she indicated by her glances. 'In there?' I said.

'Yes, sir.'

'What's up?'

She shook her head sadly, ''E keeps on calling for vittles, sir. *'Eavy* vittles 'e wants. I get 'im what I can. Pork 'e's 'ad, sooit pud-din', sossiges, noo bread. Everythink like that. Left outside, if you please, and me go away. 'E's eatin', sir, something *awful*.'

There came a piping bawl from inside the door: 'That Forma-lyn?'

'That you, Pyecraft?' I shouted, and went and banged the door.

'Tell her to go away.'

I did.

Then I could hear a curious pattering upon the door, almost like someone feeling for the handle in the dark, and Pyecraft's familiar grunts.

'It's all right,' I said, 'she's gone.'

But for a long time the door didn't open.

I heard the key turn. Then Pyecraft's voice said, 'Come in.'

I turned the handle and opened the door. Naturally I expected to see Pyecraft.

Well, you know, he wasn't there!

I never had such a shock in my life. There was his sitting-room in a state of untidy disorder, plates and dishes among the books and writing things, and several chairs overturned, but Pyecraft—

'It's all right, o' man; shut the door,' he said, and then I dis-covered him.

There he was right up close to the cornice in the corner by the door, as though someone had glued him to the ceiling. His face was anxious and angry. He panted and gesticulated. 'Shut the door,' he said. 'If that woman gets hold of it—'

I shut the door, and went and stood away from him and stared.

'If anything gives way and you tumble down,' I said, 'you'll break your neck, Pyecraft.'

'I wish I could,' he wheezed.

'A man of your age and weight getting up to kiddish gymnas-tics—'

'Don't,' he said, and looked agonized. 'Your damned great-grandmother—'

'Be careful,' I warned him.

'I'll tell you,' he said, and gesticulated.

'How the deuce,' said I, 'are you holding on up there?'

And then abruptly I realized that he was not holding on at all, that he was floating up there—just as a gas-filled bladder might have floated in the same position. He began a struggle to thrust himself away from the ceiling and to clamber down the wall to me. 'It's that prescription,' he panted, as he did so. 'Your great-gran—'

'*No!*' I cried.

He took hold of a framed engraving rather carelessly as he spoke and it gave way, and he flew back to the ceiling again, while the picture smashed on to the sofa. Bump he went against the ceiling, and I knew then why he was all over white on the more salient curves and angles of his person. He tried again more carefully, coming down by way of the mantel.

It was really a most extraordinary spectacle, that great, fat, apoplectic-looking man upside down and trying to get from the ceiling to the floor. 'That prescription,' he said. 'Too successful.'

'How?'

'Loss of weight—almost complete.'

And then, of course, I understood.

'By Jove, Pyecraft,' said I, 'what you wanted was a cure for fatness! But you always called it weight. You would call it weight.'

Somehow I was extremely delighted. I quite liked Pyecraft for the time. 'Let me help you!' I said, and took his hand and pulled him down. He kicked about, trying to get foothold somewhere. It was very like holding a flag on a windy day.

'That table,' he said, pointing, 'is solid mahogany and very heavy. If you can put me under that—'

I did, and there he wallowed about like a captive balloon, while I stood on his hearthrug and talked to him.

I lit a cigar. 'Tell me,' I said, 'what happened?'

'I took it,' he said.

'How did it taste?'

'Oh, *beastly!*'

I should fancy they all did. Whether one regards the ingredients or the probable compound or the possible results, almost all my great-grandmother's remedies appear to me at least to be extraordinarily uninviting. For my own part—

'I took a little sip first.'

'Yes?'

'And as I felt lighter and better after an hour, I decided to take the draught.'

'My dear Pyecraft!'

'I held my nose,' he explained. 'And then I kept on getting lighter and lighter—and helpless, you know.'

He gave way suddenly to a burst of passion. 'What the goodness am I to *do*?' he said.

'There's one thing pretty evident,' I said, 'that you mustn't do. If you go out of doors you'll go up and up.' I waved an arm upward. 'They'd have to send Santos-Dumont after you to bring you down again.'

'I suppose it will wear off?'

I shook my head. 'I don't think you can count on that,' I said.

And then there was another burst of passion, and he kicked out at adjacent chairs and banged the floor. He behaved just as I should have expected a great, fat, self-indulgent man to behave under trying circumstances—that is to say, very badly. He spoke of me and of my great-grandmother with an utter want of discretion.

'I never asked you to take the stuff,' I said.

And generously disregarding the insults he was putting upon me, I sat down in his armchair and began to talk to him in a sober, friendly fashion.

I pointed out to him that this was a trouble he had brought upon himself, and that it had almost an air of poetical justice. He had eaten too much. This he disputed, and for a time we argued the point.

He became noisy and violent, so I desisted from this aspect of his lesson. 'And then,' said I, 'you committed the sin of euphuism. You called it, not Fat, which is just and inglorious, but Weight. You—'

He interrupted to say that he recognized all that. What was he to *do*?

I suggested he should adapt himself to his new conditions. So we came to the really sensible part of the business. I suggested that it would not be difficult for him to learn to walk about on the ceiling with his hands—

'I can't sleep,' he said.

But that was no great difficulty. It was quite possible, I pointed out, to make a shake-up under a wire mattress, fasten the under things on with tapes, and have a blanket, sheet, and coverlid to button at the side. He would have to confide in his housekeeper, I said; and after some squabbling he agreed to that. (Afterwards it was quite delightful to see the beautifully matter-of-fact way with which the good lady took all these amazing inversions.) He could have a library ladder in his room, and all his meals could be laid on the top of his bookcase. We also hit on an ingenious device by which he could get to the floor whenever he wanted, which was simply to put the *British Encyclopaedia* (tenth edition) on the top of his open shelves. He just pulled out a couple of volumes and held on, and down he came. And we agreed there must be iron staples along the skirting, so that he could cling to those whenever he wanted to get about the room on the lower level.

As we got on with the thing I found myself almost keenly interested. It was I who called in the housekeeper and broke matters to her, and it was I chiefly who fixed up the inverted bed. In fact, I spent two whole days at his flat. I am a handy interfering sort of man with a screwdriver, and I made all sorts of ingenious adaptations for him—ran a wire to bring his bells within reach, turned all his electric lights up instead of down, and so on. The whole affair was extremely curious and interesting to me, and it was delightful to think of Pyecraft like some great, fat blow-fly, crawling about on his ceiling and clambering round the lintel of his doors from one room to another, and never, never, never coming to the club any more. . . .

Then, you know, my fatal ingenuity got the better of me. I was sitting by his fire drinking his whisky, and he was up in his favourite corner by the cornice, tacking a Turkey carpet to the ceiling, when the idea struck me. 'By Jove, Pyecraft!' I said, 'all this is totally unnecessary.'

And before I could calculate the complete consequences of my notion I blurted it out. 'Lead underclothing,' said I, and the mischief was done.

Pyecraft received the thing almost in tears. 'To be right ways up again—' he said.

I gave him the whole secret before I saw where it would take me. 'Buy sheet lead,' I said, 'stamp it into discs. Sew 'em all over your underclothes until you have enough. Have lead-soled boots, carry a bag of solid lead, and the thing is done! Instead of being a prisoner here you may go abroad again, Pyecraft! you may travel—'

A still happier idea came to me. 'You need never fear a shipwreck. All you need do is just slip off some or all of your clothes, take the necessary amount of luggage in your hand, and float up in the air—'

In his emotion he dropped the tack-hammer within an ace of

my head. 'By Jove!' he said, 'I shall be able to come back to the club again.'

The thing pulled me up short. 'By Jove!' I said, faintly. 'Yes. Of course—you will.'

He did. He does. There he sits beind me now stuffing—as I live!—a third go of buttered teacake. And no one in the whole world knows—except his housekeeper and me—that he weighs practically nothing; that he is a mere boring mass of assimilatory matters, mere clouds in clothing, *niente*, *nefas*, and most inconsiderable of men. There he sits watching until I have done this writing. Then, if he can, he will waylay me. He will come billowing up to me....

He will tell me over again all about it, how it feels, how it doesn't feel, how he sometimes hopes it is passing off a little. And always somewhere in that fat, abundant discourse he will say, 'The secret's keeping, eh? If anyone knew of it—I should be so ashamed.... Makes a fellow look such a fool, you know. Crawling about on a ceiling and all that....'

And now to elude Pyecraft, occupying, as he does, an admirable strategic position between me and the door.

Sources and
Acknowledgements

The editor wishes to thank the following authors (or their agents or trustees) and publishers who have granted permission to reproduce copyright material:

'The Flying Goat' by H. E. Bates, from *Twenty Tales* (Jonathan Cape) by permission of Laurence Pollinger and the Estate of the late H. E. Bates.

'The Burglary' by Arnold Bennett, from *The Grim Smile of the Five Towns* (Chatto and Windus) by permission of the executors of the Estate of the late Mrs Dorothy Cheston Bennett.

'Rope Enough' by John Collier, from *Presenting Moonshine* (Macmillan, London and Basingstoke) by permission of A. D. Peters.

'On a Wing and a Prayer' by Alan Coren, from *Golfing for Cats* (Robson Books).

'Tony Kytes, the Arch Deceiver' by Thomas Hardy, from *Life's Little Ironies* by permission of the Trustees of the Hardy Estate and Macmillan, London and Basingstoke.

'The Persecution of Bob Pretty' by W. W. Jacobs by permission of The Society of Authors as the literary representative of the Estate of W. W. Jacobs.

'UB' by Paul Jennings, from *Oddly Enough* by permission of The Bodley Head.

'Soaked in Seaweed' by Stephen Leacock, from *Nonsense Novels* by permission of The Bodley Head and McClelland and Stewart.

'First Confession' by Frank O'Connor, from *Stories of Frank O'Connor* (Hamish Hamilton) by permission of A. D. Peters.

'The Oompa' by Gwyn Thomas, from *The Lust Lobby* by permission of Curtis Brown.

'The Secret Life of Walter Mitty' and 'The Macbeth Murder Mystery' by James Thurber © 1942. © 1970 Helen Thurber. From *Vintage Thurber* (Hamish Hamilton) and *My World – and Welcome to it* (Harcourt Brace Jovanovich). First printed in *The New Yorker*.

'The Truth about Pyecraft' by H. G. Wells by permission of the Estate of the late H. G. Wells.